Not
Your Average
J·O·E

NOT YOUR AVERAGE J·O·E

by Michael Delaney

illustrated by Chris Burke

E. P. DUTTON   NEW YORK

I'd like to thank Don Levine, the inventor of G.I. Joe, and also John Gildea.

M.C.D.

The name G.I. Joe is used in this novel with special permission of Marvel Comics and Hasbro, Inc.

Text copyright © 1990 by M. C. Delaney
Illustrations copyright © 1990 by Chris Burke

Library of Congress Cataloging-in-Publication Data

Delaney, M. C. (Michael Clark)
  Not your average Joe / by Michael Delaney; illustrated by Chris Burke.
      p.   cm.
  Summary: Playing with her brother's old chemistry set, Nicole mixes a formula which makes her uncle's old G.I. Joe doll come alive.
  ISBN 0-525-44538-2
  [1. Dolls—Fiction.]   I. Burke, Chris, ill.   II. Title
PZ7.D37319No   1990   89-34477
[Fic]—dc20   CIP
                                             AC
Published in the United States by E. P. Dutton, a division of Penguin Books USA Inc.

Published simultaneously in Canada by Fitzhenry & Whiteside Limited, Toronto

Designer: Martha Rago

Printed in the U.S.A.   First Edition
10 9 8 7 6 5 4 3 2 1

1.

I AM AT THE KITCHEN table with a tall glass of milk and some Oreos. As I sit eating, I am looking at the *TV Guide* to see if anything good is on TV this afternoon. Nobody is home but me. The kitchen is filled with sunlight, and the house is so quiet I can hear the soft rumble of the furnace when it clicks on in the cellar.

I'm always the first one home after school. My older brother, Matthew, who is in junior high, doesn't get home till after three o'clock. Usually after school I go over to Marcia's house or Marcia comes over to mine, but today Marcia is at her piano lesson. Marcia is my best friend. We're eleven years old.

There isn't anything I particularly want to watch on TV, so after I finish my milk and cookies, I go up to the attic. It's not really an attic—it's really the third floor of our house, but we call it the attic. It's this huge room filled with all kinds of junk. Mom keeps saying she is going to clean it one of these days, but she never does. She's just too busy, she says.

Anyway, I go to the attic to look for this disguise kit. I want to find the eye patch that's in the kit, along with the fake mustache and stick-on bushy eyebrows. See, Halloween is tomorrow and I'm going out as a pirate. Nicole, the one-eyed pirate.

The only problem is, I can't find the dumb disguise kit. I was positive it was in the wooden toy chest with all the board games and jigsaw puzzles, but it's not.

While I'm rummaging around in the toy chest, I discover this Mr. Chemistry set that Matthew got one Christmas a few years ago. The cardboard box that the set came in smells a little musty when I open it up. There are all these very intriguing test tubes, eyedroppers, beakers, and little bottles that are partly filled with colored chemicals and powders. There's even a white scientist's apron. I tie the strings of the apron around my waist, and then I

begin to mix a little of this chemical with a little of that chemical in a beaker.

I'm just fooling around, pretending I'm Madame Curie, who discovered radium. I have to write a dumb science report on Madame Curie for my homework assignment, that's why I'm thinking of her. After I've mixed the chemicals, I try to think of what else I can put in. I trot down to the bathroom on the second floor, and add a few drops of Pepto-Bismol, a half capful of mint mouthwash, a squirt of shaving cream, a teeny bit of Head & Shoulders shampoo, and just a smidgen of toothpaste with MFP flouride. I return to the attic, where I delicately pour a small amount of my formula into a test tube. I swoosh it around, wondering what I should do with the stuff, when I see a bunch of old dolls on the windowsill. Barbie, Ken, G.I. Joe, and some other dolls are standing there with their backs against the glass.

"Well, hello," I say cheerfully, as I walk over and pick up the G.I. Joe doll. It's one of those very old G.I. Joe's that's about a foot high. He has this little man's face, with a bad scar on his left cheek. The doll used to be my uncle's when he was growing up. "You look like you could use a bit of radium."

I lift the test tube to the G.I. Joe's lips; my formula dribbles down his chin and onto his olive-green fatigues. "Poor guy," I say, shaking my head as I set the G.I. Joe back on the windowsill. "Even radium can't help him."

Just then, I hear voices coming from the heating duct across the room. I creep over to it, squat, and listen. It's Matthew and two of his friends, Stringbean and Eric Fischer. They're down in the kitchen. The three of them are in a rock band, the Dead Batteries, and Mom lets them practice in our attic. Which means there's a good chance they might be coming up to the attic soon. The last thing I want is for Matthew to see me pretending to be Madame Curie. If he does, he'll never leave me alone. Matthew loves to tease me.

So I hurry down the attic stairs and slip back into the second floor bathroom. I flush the remains of my formula down the toilet. Then I rinse out the test tube and beaker, like a good little mad scientist, and dry them off with a towel.

I return to the attic and put the test tube and beaker back into the Mr. Chemistry set. As I'm undoing the apron, I hear a small thud over by the window where the dolls are. I look over, but I can't figure out what fell. It's pretty windy outside—maybe a small branch from the tree outside the window broke and dropped onto the roof?

I don't know why, but something feels strange. Very strange. I'm still staring at the window when I realize what it is.

The G.I. Joe isn't on the windowsill—or anywhere on the floor.

2.

ALL OF A SUDDEN I get this creepy feeling that I'm being watched. I swing around—just in time to see a little head disappear behind the trunk I always take with me to summer camp. It's the G.I. Joe!

I do what any scientist would do: I shriek.

The G.I. Joe leaps out from behind the trunk, and I shriek again. He dashes jerkily across the floor and dives behind Matthew's guitar amplifier. My heart pounds as I inch over to the drum set. Two drumsticks are resting on the snare drum. I pick one up and chuck it toward the amplifier. The G.I. Joe springs out and runs across the floor, first in one direction, then in another. There is a golf bag with golf clubs in it lying on the floor. The G.I. Joe races over and vanishes inside it.

I grab an old ski pole and try to poke him out, but it's too dark inside the golf bag to see him. A cardboard carton filled with a string of Christmas lights is in the corner of the room. I go over, dump the lights out, walk quietly back, and stand over the golf bag. I stomp my feet and give it a couple of good, hard kicks.

The second the G.I. Joe scrambles out, *whammo,* I drop the carton over him. The G.I. Joe is beating his little fists against the side of the carton. Mom's old iron is sitting on a stack of magazines. I reach over and plop the iron down on the carton.

I'm so excited, all I can do is stand there, panting, bent over with my hands on my knees. As soon as I catch my breath, I rush down to Mom's bedroom, where there's a phone on the small table beside her bed. Mulligan, our gray-striped tiger cat, is sitting on the white bedspread on top of Mom's pillow. I call Marcia. I'm hoping—praying—she'll be home from her piano lesson.

Her little brother, Petey, answers. "Hello, this is Petey Schwartz speaking. May I help you, please?" He always answers the phone like that. Mrs. Schwartz taught him to say that, I guess.

"Hi, Petey, is Marcia there?"

Off in the distance, I hear Mrs. Schwartz yell out, "Who's the phone for?"

"Marcia!" Petey yells back—right in my ear.

I hear an extension phone lift up. "Hello?" says Mrs. Schwartz.

"Hi, Mrs. Schwartz, is Marcia there?"

"Oh, hello, Nicole. No, she's still at her piano lesson."

"Oh, she is," I say disappointedly.

"Is everything okay, Nicole? You sound out of breath."

"Everything is fine," I assure her. "Could you please ask her to call me when she gets in?"

"Bye, Nicole," says Petey abruptly. I forgot he was still there.

"Bye, Petey," I say.

"Bye, Mommy," he says.

Mrs. Schwartz and I laugh. "Bye, Petey," she says. She waits until Petey hangs up, then says, "I'll tell Marcia to call you the second she walks in the door."

"That'd be great," I reply.

We say good-bye, and hang up. I sure wish Marcia had been home. I'm dying to have her come over and see the G.I. Joe doll.

I'm in such a hurry to get back up to the attic that, as I'm stepping out into the hallway, I nearly plow into Matthew, who's on his way into his bedroom. Stringbean and Eric are just behind him.

7

"Hey!" exclaims Matthew. "What are you doing wearing my button?"

He means his button that says: STOP THE ARMS RACE, NOT THE HUMAN RACE. I borrowed it this morning without asking him. I meant to put it back on his bureau before he got home from school, but I forgot.

"I just borrowed it," I say.

"Who said you could borrow it?"

"I would've asked you, but you'd already left for school."

"A likely story," says Stringbean, who is very tall and thin.

"That's my button," says Matthew. "*My* button!"

Eric leans forward and, peering over the top of his glasses, examines the button. "That's his button, all right."

"Well, I'm sorry. I really didn't think you'd mind," I say to Matthew.

"Well, I do mind," he says. "And who gave you permission to go into my room?"

"Don't look at me," says Stringbean.

"Or me," says Eric.

"I said I was sorry, Matthew. Here," I say, taking the button off. I toss it at him. "Take your dumb old button."

I start to walk away when Eric grabs me from behind. "Not so fast," he says.

"Hey, come on, cut it out," Matthew says and pulls Eric from me.

The phone rings. I start to go into Mom's bedroom to answer it, but Matthew hurries in and beats me to the phone.

"Petruzzi's Morgue," he says into the receiver. "You kill 'em, we chill 'em." He listens. "I'm sorry, but you must have the wrong number. There's no Marcia living here. Oh, *you're* Marcia!" He knows perfectly well who Marcia is—he's just trying to be funny. "You want *who*?" he asks. "*Nicole?* Why on earth do you want to speak to *her*? Why would anyone in their right mind want to speak to *her*?"

I step forward, holding out my hand, palm up. "May I please have the phone?"

"Just a sec, Marcia," he says. "I'll go let her out of her cage."

"Very funny," I say, taking the phone from him. I wait until he and his two friends leave, and then I stick my tongue out at him. He makes me so mad sometimes.

3.

"HELLO, MARCIA?" I say.

"Oh, brother!" Marcia blurts out at the other end. "You won't believe what just happened to me."

"You won't believe what just happened to *me*!" I say. "I was up in the attic and—"

"I just found out I got a chain letter!" wails Marcia. "A chain letter that came in the mail *last* week!"

"Huh," I say. "So, anyway, there I was up in the attic, right, when—"

"See, my mom put the letter on my desk," Marcia says. "Right next to my piggy bank. But because of all the junk on my desk, I didn't see it until just a couple of minutes ago when I was putting in that really old penny I found this morning. I guess that'll teach me to clean up my desk."

"I guess so," I say, doing my best to be patient. I

hop onto Mom's bed and scratch Mulligan behind his ear. "Now wait till you hear what just happened to me."

"Oh, geez Louise!" moans Marcia. "What am I going to do?"

"Look, Marcia, I wouldn't worry about it."

"Well of course you wouldn't—*you* haven't heard what it says. Here, listen to this." She starts to read the chain letter to me. " 'This letter has been sent to you for good luck. It has been around the world twelve times. The luck has been sent to you. You will receive the luck within four days after receiving this letter—providing you don't break the chain. You must make twenty copies and send them to twenty of your friends. This is no joke!' " (Marcia groans.) " 'Do *not* keep this letter! It *must* leave your hands within forty-eight hours. An RAF officer received twenty-five thousand dollars but lost it all because he only sent out seventeen letters. Constantino Diaz ignored this letter, and six racketeers roughed him up and left him in a garbage dumpster.' " (Marcia groans again.) " 'Do not let this sort of bad luck happen to you. Send out twenty copies of this letter within forty-eight hours.' " Marcia pauses a moment. "That's the end of the letter," she says, with a worried sigh. "What am I going to do? *I'm doomed!*"

"Marcia," I say. "You're not doomed. It's only a dumb letter. Forget about it."

11

"Forget about it, she says. That's easy for you to say, Nicole. You didn't break the chain."

"Even if I had gotten the letter, I wouldn't worry about it. I really wouldn't. Look, Marcia, you and I have been through a lot together. I mean, I don't know *what* I would've done without you when my dad moved out of our house. I really don't. And I'm going to be right by your side if anything should happen to you on account of this dumb chain letter— which I seriously doubt. So come on, don't worry about it."

Marcia isn't even listening to me. "Twelve times around the world, and *I* have to break it!" she says.

"Marcia, you haven't listened to a word I've said."

"I bet a UFO kidnaps me," declares Marcia. "How much do you want to bet that's what happens?"

"That's not going to happen and you know it," I am telling her when, through the open door of Mom's bedroom, I see Matthew and his friends walk by, heading toward the back stairs. Matthew has a football under his arm. "Now, can I please tell you what just happened to me?"

"Hey!" cries Marcia. "You think I'd still get bad luck if I sent twenty letters now?"

"Marcia!" I all but scream. Frightened, Mulligan leaps off Mom's bed and runs out of the room.

"What are you trying to do?" says Marcia. "Damage my eardrum or something?"

"I'm sorry, but you're not listening to me. You have to come over to my house right this minute. Something really weird just happened."

"*What?*"

"Just get over here, quick!" I say, and hang up.

4.

Marcia lives down the street, so it takes her no time at all to get over to my house.

"So what happened?" she asks excitedly, as she comes into the kitchen. I open up the dishwasher and pull out the bottom rack. Matthew, Stringbean, and Eric are in the backyard, heaving the football back and forth to one another. I can see them out the kitchen window.

"Here," I say. "You'll need this." I hand her this big frying pan.

Marcia, who wears glasses and has sort of frizzy reddish-brown hair, stares at the frying pan. "Why will I need this?"

"We may have to clunk it over the head," I say, walking over to the broom closet.

"Clunk *what* over the head?"

"If I told you, you wouldn't believe me," I answer, taking out a broom.

"I'll believe you," she says.

I shake my head. "No, you won't."

"Well, where is it?" she asks as she follows me up the stairs to the bedroom hallway.

"In the attic."

"The attic? It isn't a mouse, is it?" Marcia asks in alarm. "Because if it is, Nicole, I'd rather not have anything to do—"

"It's not a mouse," I say as we start up the narrow staircase that leads up to the attic. "I *wish* it was a mouse."

"What do you mean by *that*?"

I turn, pressing my finger to my lips. "Shhh!"

"I sure wish you'd tell me what's going on," she whispers.

Although it isn't that late in the afternoon, the clocks were turned back over the weekend, and the light in the attic is now so dim and shadowy I have to flick on the lights. "It's under that box," I say, pointing.

"Would you please tell me what's under there?" Marcia pleads.

"Just stand behind the box," I instruct her. I don't mean to be so pushy, but I'm nervous. "And get your frying pan ready."

Marcia, clutching the handle in both hands, raises the frying pan above her head. "I'm going to kill you, Nicole, if nothing is under there."

Very slowly, I lift the iron off the carton. Glancing

15

at Marcia, I whisper, "Here goes nothing." With the straw part of the broom, I flip over the carton.

The G.I. Joe is anxiously pacing around in a circle. His hands are clasped behind his back. He looks up at me, surprised, then whirls around and starts to run—straight at Marcia. Marcia leaps back, screaming. The G.I. Joe leaps back, screaming. He whirls around again and starts to make a beeline for the golf bag, but I slam the broom down right in front of him, missing him by inches. He belly flops to the floor, covering his head with his hands. I hold the broom above him, ready to swat him if he tries to flee again.

"What are you waiting for?" Marcia cries. "Kill it! Kill it!"

I'm scared, but I'm also fascinated. "Look at him, Marcia. Isn't he amazing? It's a G.I. Joe doll!"

"Oh, brother!" Marcia groans. "I *knew* something bad was going to happen because I broke that chain letter! I just knew it!"

I kneel down so I can get a better look at the G.I. Joe. He peeks up at me from under his arm. He looks absolutely terrified.

"Didn't I tell you something bad was going to happen?" wails Marcia. "I wish, I *wish* I'd never gotten that dumb old chain letter!"

I start to reach my hand out to touch the G.I. Joe when Marcia shrieks, *"What are you doing?"*

I pull my hand back, fast. "I was just going to touch him!"

"Are you out of your mind?" Marcia exclaims. "What if he tries to bite you? What if he has rabies?"

I hadn't thought of that. "Look, if he tries anything, let him have it."

Marcia lifts the frying pan and steps bravely forward. "Okay, go!" she commands.

I quickly reach over, touch the G.I. Joe on the back, then yank my hand away. I wait a moment for my heart to stop pounding, and then I touch him again. This time I leave my hand on his back a little longer. "Boy, you should feel him," I say. "He's trembling like crazy."

"Some G.I. Joe *he* is," scoffs Marcia, who is still holding the frying pan, all set to clobber him if he makes one false move.

"Poor guy," I say. "He's so scared. I wonder what we can do to calm him down."

Marcia sets the frying pan on the floor beside me.

17

"I have a thought," she says and hurries toward the door.

"Where are you going?"

"I'll be right back."

"Hey, don't leave me here all by myself!" I call out, alarmed, but she's already disappeared down the attic stairs.

While I wait for Marcia to return, I watch the G.I. Joe. Gathering my courage, I touch him on the neck, just below his painted brown hair. His skin feels plastic like a doll's, but it also feels soft and warm like a real person's.

It gives me the creeps.

5.

ABOUT A MILLION years later, Marcia finally returns to the attic, her arms filled with food. She has a small carton of milk, a box of Froot Loops, an uncooked hot dog, a box of graham crackers, a jar of peanut butter, a bag of marshmallows, a head of lettuce, a bottle of chocolate syrup, a box of Ring Dings, and a jar of apple sauce. She also has brought some napkins and a stack of small paper cups.

"What's all this for?" I ask.

Marcia dumps everything on the floor. "I thought if we fed him, maybe he wouldn't be so scared of us."

"Hey, good thinking," I say.

"Here. Give him this first," says Marcia, sitting down. She hands me a Ring Ding. "If he has any brains, he'll love it." Ring Dings are Marcia's favorite things to eat. Actually, although I would never tell her this, *I* think Marcia should lay off the Ring Dings. She's kind of on the plump side. I unwrap the foil and place a little piece of the small cupcake on the palm of my hand, and then I stick my hand out in front of the G.I. Joe's face. He stares at it, looking very bewildered.

"Go on," I say encouragingly. "It's for you."

"You'll love it," says Marcia.

The G.I. Joe sits up and looks at me. I smile. He turns his head and looks at Marcia. Marcia points to the piece of Ring Ding in my hand. "Eat!" she says firmly. She breaks off another piece of the Ring Ding and pops it into her mouth. She makes these big, exaggerated chomps. She gulps. "Yum-yum!" she exclaims, patting her stomach.

"Boy, do you look dumb," I say.

Marcia points to the G.I. Joe doll. "Look!"

The G.I. Joe has stuck his hand into the white fluffy cream that's on the piece of Ring Ding. Cautiously, he puts his hand to his mouth and licks it.

His face brightens. He eagerly picks up the piece of Ring Ding with both hands and takes a big bite. Then he takes another big bite. Then another. He has Ring Ding all over his face.

"He likes it!" I say excitedly.

"Hey, he's no dummy!" says Marcia.

"Look at him," I say. "He's starving."

Marcia offers him more of the Ring Ding. Then she picks up a paper cup and begins to tear it along the edge.

"Marcia," I say. "I could be wrong, but I seriously doubt he's going to like paper cups."

"I'm just making him a little cup to drink from," she explains. She rips off the top half of the cup. Then she pours a small amount of chocolate syrup into the cup, and adds milk, polishing off the carton. She stirs the milk with her pinky until it turns chocolate brown, and then she licks her pinky. She is about to give the cup to the G.I. Joe when I say, "I'll do it." I take the cup from her and place it, delicately, in front of the G.I. Joe.

"Drink!" orders Marcia. She takes an empty paper cup, toasts Joe, then brings it to her lips, pretending to drink. The G.I. Joe watches her in fascination. Then he, too, raises his paper cup, toasts Marcia, and takes a sip. His eyes grow large. He drinks the whole thing in one gulp.

"I think he likes it," says Marcia.

"I'll say," I reply. I pick up a napkin and, reaching over slowly so as not to scare the G.I. Joe, I wipe off the tiny chocolate mustache that has formed above his upper lip.

The G.I. Joe points to the Ring Ding.

"You want more?" I ask, pointing to the Ring Ding.

He nods, still pointing.

"Boy," I say to Marcia as I break off another small piece. "He certainly is a little piggo."

"You know," says Marcia. "He's kind of cute. It's too bad he has that awful scar on his cheek."

"It's funny," I tell Marcia, "but whenever I used to play with him, I always made believe he was this real tough guy who wasn't afraid of anything. This G.I. Joe isn't anything like that."

"I know what you mean," agrees Marcia. "He doesn't seem very brave for an army guy, does he? Say, what if we just called him Joe?"

"Joe?" I reply. "Sure. That's okay with me."

Marcia, beaming, points to the G.I. Joe. "You Joe!" she says to him in this Tarzan-like voice. Then she points to herself. "Me Marcia!" Then she points to me. "She Nicole!"

6.

I'D FORGOTTEN THAT Matthew and his friends were home until Matthew yells out from downstairs, "Hey, Nicole!"

"What?" I yell back.

I hear his footsteps, loud and heavy, on the attic stairs. Marcia, Joe, and I all turn toward the door.

"Hey, Nicole, what did you do with the bicycle pump? The football needs air," he says, appearing at the top of the attic stairs. He looks hot and sweaty.

"I don't know where it is," I answer.

Joe looks frightened. He stands up, his eyes fixed on Matthew.

"You're the last one who used it," says Matthew. Then he spots Joe and does a double take. "Whoa!" he says incredulously. "How are you doing that?"

"Doing what?" I ask as if I have no idea what he is talking about.

"Making that G.I. Joe doll move around like that."

I look at Joe. He looks at me. "I'm not doing a thing."

"Tell me, really. How are you doing that?"

"I told you. I'm not doing a thing," I say again.

"He's doing it all by himself," says Marcia proudly.

Matthew regards us suspiciously. "Get out of here!"

"He is!" I insist.

Matthew kneels down in front of Joe. He taps his fingers on the floor, an inch or so from where Joe is standing. Joe squats and taps *his* fingers on the floor.

"Would someone please tell me what is going on here?" says Matthew.

Marcia throws me a glance and then confesses, "I broke a chain letter and the G.I. Joe came to life."

"A *chain letter*?" exclaims Matthew, baffled.

Marcia says, "Can you believe it?"

"I found him," I say.

"Up here in the attic?"

"Yeah. He used to be on the windowsill over there."

"And you found him just like this? I mean, alive?"

I nod. "Yeah."

Matthew has this nervous tic near the side of his mouth that twitches whenever he gets excited about something. It's twitching now. "This is awesome," he says. "Really awesome. Boy, he's just like a real person, but he's a G.I. Joe doll."

"He's not your average G.I. Joe, that's for sure," I say, making a pun on that expression, not your average Joe. It's something Dad used to say about Matthew. This was when Dad still lived with us, before he and Mom got divorced. Whenever Matthew did something nobody else could do, you know, like wiggle his ears or something, Dad would say, "Well, I always knew he wasn't your average Joe!" Dad has a lot of funny expressions like that. But nobody laughs at my joke. "Get it?" I ask. "Not your average Joe. Not your average *G.I.* Joe."

Marcia groans.

"Hey, G.I. Joe," Matthew says.

"You can call him Joe," says Marcia.

Joe and Matthew stare at each other. Finally, Joe points to the last little piece of Ring Ding. He has this happy expression on his face. He rubs his stomach like Marcia did.

"Hey, look!" says Matthew in amazement. "He's pointing to this Ring Ding." Matthew picks up the piece of Ring Ding. "Thanks, big guy. Don't mind if I do."

Joe's face falls as Matthew pops the piece of Ring Ding into his mouth.

"I think he wanted you to feed him," Marcia says in a small voice.

"This is awesome!" repeats Matthew. "Totally awesome! He's so human! I wonder how human he really is. I know. Let's see if he's ticklish."

"No!" Marcia and I both cry out at once.

Too late. Matthew has picked up Joe. He wiggles his finger in Joe's armpit. Joe, squirming, bursts into tiny peals of shrill laughter.

"Excellent!" says Matthew, stopping. "He passes the ticklish test with flying colors. Now for the light-socket test."

"No!" I scream, and grab Joe from his hand.

"Oh, Nicole, I was only kidding," Matthew says scornfully. "I wasn't really going to do that."

He may say that, but I don't trust him. Matthew can be pretty mean sometimes.

I set Joe on the floor and pat him on the head. "I wouldn't put it past you," I say to Matthew. "Not for a second."

"I told you I wasn't going to do it. Don't be such an old stick-in-the-mud."

"I'm not an old stick-in-the-mud."

"You are! Old Stick-in-the-Mud Petruzzi," he says.

"Shut up, Matthew!"

"We should've named you Stick-in-the-Mud instead of Nicole. Then we could've called you 'Mud' for short."

I lose my temper then and try to slug him. Matthew grabs my fist and, in a flash, wrestles me down to the floor. He pins my arms down with his knees.

"You big dumb jerk!" I shout.

"Take it back!" he demands.

"No!" I answer.

"You take it back!"

"No!" I say again. "You're so dumb, you can barely get C's."

"Take it back or I'll sit on you till I break every rib in your body." He is sitting right on top of my chest.

"Yeah, right!" I say, sarcastic as anything.

"Are you going to take it back?"

I can hardly breathe. Marcia is pleading with me to just do what he says, for crying out loud.

"No, I won't take it back!"

Matthew sits even heavier on me. "I said, take it—OW!" he suddenly screams and leaps off me. He bends down and pulls up the left leg of his jeans. There is a tiny red mark above his ankle. Matthew points a finger at Joe, saying, "He bit me! The little twerp bit me!"

I prop myself up on my elbows and gaze at Joe. He is down by my feet, looking warily up at Matthew. He is breathing so hard his little chest is heaving. I'm surprised and touched that he came to my rescue.

Matthew stomps his foot as if he were about to come after Joe.

Joe, petrified, rushes to my side.

7.

I PICK JOE UP and scramble to my feet. "Come on, Marcia, let's go."

"Just let me get this stuff," she says. She is on her knees, hastily picking up all the food.

"I can't believe he bit me," scowls Matthew as he massages his ankle.

"Let's go, Marcia!" I say.

"I am!" she replies. She is having difficulty carrying everything. The jar of peanut butter keeps dropping out of her arms.

Matthew pulls up his sock and lowers his pant leg. "I swear, if that little twerp ever tries that stunt again, I'm going to put him in a food processor—on chop. Then mince."

"Yeah, right," I say, trying to sound tough. Actually, he's making me very nervous. "Marcia, would you forget the dumb food and just come!" I turn and run down the attic stairs, two steps at a time.

"I'm coming! I'm coming! Geez Louise!" says Marcia, as she comes bounding down after me.

As soon as Marcia is in my bedroom, I close the door and lock it. Marcia dumps all the food onto my bed, and I set Joe down on top of my desk. "That was a very brave thing you did just now in the attic—" I am saying, but Joe isn't listening. He walks right over to the edge of the desk and stops, looking eagerly around my room. He leans forward and peers at the fish tank that is on a little table beside my desk. Tropical fish are swimming about in the greenish water. "Well," I say to Marcia, who is sitting on my bed, unwrapping a Ring Ding. "So much for trying to thank Joe."

Marcia bites into the Ring Ding. With her mouth full, she replies, "Oh well, what can you do?"

Turning, Joe spots a pencil on my green blotter. He picks it up and holds it in the middle, the way you'd carry a long board.

"Hey, Joe, let me sharpen that for you," I offer, but Joe won't let go of the pencil. "Okay, *you* can sharpen it." I pick up my electric pencil sharpener and set it down before Joe. Then I help him stick in the pencil.

Vrrrr! whirs the pencil sharpener.

Joe lets out a startled cry and leaps back.

"It's okay, Joe," I say soothingly. "It won't hurt you. Go on—try it again."

I give him a little nudge toward the pencil. He timidly lifts the pencil and pushes it into the pencil sharpener.

Vrrrr . . . vrrrrrr . . . vrrrrrrrrrrrrrrrrrrrr!

"That's enough," I say.

Vrrrrrrrrrrrrrrrrrrrrrrrrrrr!

"You can stop now, Joe," I say. "See, it's sharp." I pull the pencil out of the pencil sharpener and touch the point to show him.

But Joe isn't the least bit interested if it's sharp or not. He just likes sharpening pencils. He puts the pencil back into the pencil sharpener. *Vrrr! Vrrr! Vrrrrrrrrrrr!* He just keeps sharpening and sharpening it.

"Looks like Joe has found a hobby," observes Marcia.

"I guess so," I say, laughing.

I open my bottom desk drawer and grab a bunch of pencils that are in an old cigar box. "Good thing I have tons of them," I say as I place the pencils beside Joe so that as soon as he finishes with one pencil he can begin to sharpen another. I realize that at the rate Joe is sharpening, the pencil sharpener will be filled with shavings in no time flat. So I pull out the drawer that holds the pencil shavings and dump it into my wastebasket.

While Joe is sharpening pencils, Marcia and I make him a home. After a somewhat lengthy discussion as to whether we should use the old canary cage up in the attic ("The poor little guy will think he's behind bars!" cries Marcia.), we decide to use the aquarium where I used to keep my gerbil, Mr. Higglebee, until he died. We use a shoe box as a bed, with two big sponges for a mattress. The sponges are a little on the stiff side, so I go to the top drawer of my bureau and take out some of Dad's old handkerchiefs to place over the sponges. Then Marcia makes Joe's bed up, using little bathroom towels for covers.

To make the place look homey, we put in antique doll furniture that belonged to my grandmother when she was a little girl. Mom has it packed in a carton that she keeps on a shelf in her bedroom closet. We put in a braided oval rug, a big green stuffed chair, a floor lamp (which Marcia places beside the chair), and a bureau with a mirror attached to it. I place an itty-bitty comb on top of the bureau, just in case Joe ever feels like combing his hair.

"Well, Joe, how do you like your new home?" I ask.

Joe is so busy sharpening a pencil, he doesn't even hear me.

"Here, Joe, let's try out your new home," I say and pick him up. I am about to set him in the aquarium when someone jiggles my doorknob.

"Hey, Nicole, open up!" Matthew's voice calls out. "I want to show Stringbean and Eric the G.I. Joe."

"Go away!" I tell him. I place Joe beside me on the floor.

Then Stringbean's voice says, "Boy, Matt, you must think we're a couple of real numbskulls to think we'd actually believe a G.I. Joe came to life."

"But one did!" insists Matthew. "Come on, Nicole, open up!"

"Leave us alone!" I say.

"Yeah," says Marcia.

"Look, I'll let you wear my button," says Matthew.

"Yeah, right," I answer.

"Hey, Matt!" cries Eric. "I think I just saw a leprechaun run into your bedroom!"

"Very funny," replies Matthew. He jiggles my doorknob again. "Would you open up, Nicole!" I can tell he's getting very impatient.

"Go away and leave us alone!"

"Some sister *you* are!" Matthew hits the door, hard, with his fist. We hear footsteps marching up the attic stairs. About a minute later, there is a loud *thuuuuuuuuuummmmm!* Then a *thum! Thum!*

32

Thum! Thum! Thum! Thum! It is Matthew, playing his electric bass guitar. The entire house vibrates with every *thum!*

"I guess it's band-practice time," I sigh.

"How can you live with that noise?" Marcia asks in disgust.

I tap Marcia on the arm and point to Joe. He is staring, perplexed, up at the ceiling. He doesn't know what the heck is going on. Every time there's a *thum!* he cocks his head in a different direction.

Marcia and I fall backwards on the floor, laughing. He looks at us. He cocks his head again, and we laugh even harder. Marcia points to the ceiling and rolls her eyes. Joe rolls *his* eyes. He looks so cute, Marcia and I can't stop laughing. Joe cocks his head and rolls his eyes again and again. I get the feeling he's doing it now only because he knows we like it.

Suddenly there is the sharp twang of an electric guitar (Stringbean), followed by a violent burst of drums (Eric). Joe is so terrified, he makes a running dive for Marcia's lap.

"Oh, the poor thing!" Marcia says, smiling, as she comforts him.

I look on, hurt. I'm jealous Joe went to Marcia, not to me.

8.

AT QUARTER AFTER six, Mom comes home from work. From outside my bedroom door, she yells out, "Matthew, it's too loud!" Then she taps on my door. "Nicole?" she says.

"Just a sec, Mom," I say, springing to my feet.

Marcia is sitting on the floor, legs crossed, playing with a little plastic kangaroo toy that does back flips when you wind it up. We've been trying to teach Joe—without much success—to do back flips.

"Hide Joe," I whisper to Marcia. I don't want Mom to come in and be startled by Joe. I figure I should break the news about Joe to her gently. I open my science book and lay it on the floor, and then I scatter some notebook pages around to make Mom think that Marcia and I have been busy doing homework. I glance at Marcia to see if she's hidden Joe yet and if it's okay to open the door. She nods.

"Hi, Hon," Mom says when I let her in. She gives me a kiss. She's wearing a long, navy blue skirt and a white blouse, and her black hair is pulled back with a silver clip. "Hello, Marcia."

"Hi, Mrs. Petruzzi," says Marcia.

"You girls are going to ruin your eyes studying in this light," Mom says disapprovingly. She walks over to the bureau and snaps on the lamp beside my jewelry box.

"What's all this food doing in your bedroom?" Mom asks. "What's this *hot dog* doing here? You know you're not supposed to have food upstairs."

"I know. I'll put it back," I say, and then I quickly change the subject. "So how was work?"

Mom switches on my desk lamp. "Work was fine," she says. She points to the pile of pencils that Joe sharpened. "What's with all the pencil stubs?"

"Nothing. Just sharpening pencils," I reply.

"How was school?" Mom asks, and plops down into my reading chair.

Marcia gasps.

"Good," I answer, glancing at her. Eyes wide open, Marcia is biting her bottom lip as she stares at Mom. "I got an A minus on my book report." I had to give an oral book report on *Anne of Green Gables* in English class.

"That's great!" exclaims Mom, crossing her legs.

Marcia squirms and wrings her hands.

"I should've gotten an A."

"Why didn't you?"

"Mrs. Hirshman said I shouldn't have spent so much time discussing the author. I should've just talked about the book."

Marcia is still wringing her hands. It is very distracting.

"Well, sorry about that," says Mom. It was Mom's suggestion that I tell the class about Lucy Maud Montgomery, the author of *Anne of Green Gables*.

I wouldn't have told Mom about the A (because I knew she'd only feel bad about it) except that Marcia is making me nervous and I'm not thinking clearly. She keeps squirming around and wringing her hands. And now she's making all these really weird little noises. I give her a what-is-your-problem? face, but she is looking at Mom and doesn't see me.

"Are you okay, Marcia?" asks Mom.

"What's that, Mrs. Petruzzi?"

I stare at Marcia. She has a squeamish look on her face, as if she were watching a science film of a snake swallowing a frog. I can't figure out what her problem is. Then I do. "Mom, quick, get up!" I cry. "You can't sit there!"

Mom stands up. "Why not?" she asks, looking down at the chair.

I lift up the seat cushion. I feel like murdering Marcia. I really do. Of all the places she could've hidden Joe, she chose to put him under the seat cushion of my reading chair.

Joe is lying in a daze on the seat of the chair. Mom picks him up. Joe blinks and shakes his head and moves his arms.

Mom lets out a horrified gasp and flings Joe up into the air. He lands with a *flop!* in my wastebasket—which, luckily, is filled with garbage.

Both Marcia and I rush over to him. "Poor Joe!" I exclaim.

"Don't touch it!" cries Mom sharply.

"It's okay," I tell her. I reach in and pull Joe out from the crumpled notebook papers and pencil shavings and Kleenexes. I wipe some pencil shavings from his hair and clothes.

"My God, it's alive!" declares Mom.

"Isn't he neat?" I ask.

"Let your mom hold him," says Marcia.

"I don't want to hold him," says Mom tensely.

"But he won't hurt you. See," I say as I hand her Joe. I can tell she's really scared of him. She holds Joe in both palms, with her arms stretched out.

"This is incredible!" Mom says. "Absolutely incredible!"

Joe looks at Mom and cocks his head. Mom nervously smiles. He cocks his head again. Then he rolls his eyes. Mom laughs. Joe rolls his eyes again. Boy, what a ham, I think.

"It's Uncle Greg's old G.I. Joe," I explain, taking Joe from her.

"Not your average G.I. Joe, that's for sure," says Marcia, with a little laugh.

I stare at Marcia. I can't believe her. She stole *my* joke. I didn't even think she liked it. "Look," I say to Mom as I set Joe down in his aquarium. "I made him a home."

"*We* made him a home," corrects Marcia.

Mom kneels and peers at Joe. She clicks her red fingernails against the aquarium glass. Joe steps up to the glass and rolls his eyes. "Where was he?" asks Mom.

"In the attic," I reply.

"*Our* attic?"

"Yes, I told you. It's Uncle Greg's old G.I. Joe doll." Mom's so nervous, she must not have heard me before.

"This is *my* brother's G.I. Joe doll? Nooo!"

"Yes!"

"It can't be!"

"It is!"

"Gosh, I wonder how he got like this," says Mom.

Marcia pipes in, "It's because I broke a chain letter."

I turn to Marcia, saying, "That's not why it happened."

"It is so," she insists.

I shake my head. "No, it isn't. It happened because I gave him this formula I made with Matthew's old chemistry set."

"Are you sure?" asks Marcia.

"Positive."

Mom asks, "What was in this formula?"

"Yeah, what was in it?" demands Marcia, skeptically, placing her hands on her hips.

I shrug. "A bunch of stuff. Some chemicals that came with the set, a little bit of Pepto-Bismol, a little bit of mouthwash. Let's see. . . ." I can't seem to remember. For some reason, my mind is a blank. I hate when that happens. "Oh, I know, some Head & Shoulders."

"How long after you gave the G.I. Joe doll this formula did he come alive?" asks Mom.

"Gee, I don't know. A couple of minutes."

"Then what happened?" Mom asks.

"He was so scared, he started running all around the floor."

Mom is quiet for a moment. She can't seem to take her eyes off Joe. Finally she says, "I'm trying to think what we should do with him."

"What do you mean?" I ask.

"Well, we can't keep him."

"Why not?"

"Well, we don't know the first thing about him. I mean, for all we know, he may have something

39

wrong with him or he may have a violent streak in him or who knows what."

"He's as harmless as a fly!" I protest.

"I don't even know what you'd feed a G.I. Joe doll."

"Oh, he likes everything," I assure her.

"Especially Ring Dings," adds Marcia.

"Suppose Mulligan attacks him the way he attacked Mr. Higglebee?" Mom asks. That's how poor Mr. Higglebee died. He escaped from his aquarium one morning and Mulligan attacked him. That's the only time I've ever hit Mulligan.

"I'll make sure that doesn't happen. Honest. Please let me keep him," I plead. *"Please!"* Hearing how awful I sound begging, I stop. "I'll take good care of him. I promise."

"Nicole, we're not talking about a gerbil or a fish from a pet store."

"I know we aren't," I answer.

Mom stands up. "Well, let's go down to the kitchen. I need to think about all of this. I mean, this is incredible. We can talk about it while we make dinner."

Marcia peers at the clock radio that's on my night table. The green illuminated numerals say 6:48. "Whoa!" she exclaims. "I've got to go!"

I walk her to the front door. As she is sticking her arm into the sleeve of her red parka, she says, "If

40

your mom won't let you keep Joe, I know my mom will."

"Don't worry," I say. "*She'll* let me keep him."

Marcia wraps her plaid scarf around her neck once, twice. She reaches into her coat pocket and pulls out a ratty-looking hat that her grandmother knitted for her. It looks about a hundred years old and it's got a dumb pom-pom. The worst part is, it's got all these

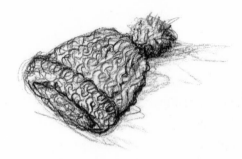

white hairs from her dog stuck to it. I must have dropped about a million hints that she looks really stupid in it, but does she ever catch on? No.

Marcia opens the front door. A cardboard skeleton is hanging on the outside of the door. "Hey, I'm out of here!"

9.

I'M CLOSING the front door when I hear Matthew's voice in the kitchen. "Yo, Mom!" he says.

"Hello, Matthew," replies Mom. "How is the band practice going?"

"Excellent," he says.

"How was school?"

Matthew groans. "Don't ask."

I take a seat on the front hallway stairs. I don't want to go into the kitchen when Matthew is there. I really don't. I hear the refrigerator door open.

"Don't eat now," says Mom. "Dinner is in half an hour."

The refrigerator door smacks closed. "It's okay," Matthew says. "I'm not eating here."

I feel something rub up against my back and, turning, I find Mulligan. He's purring loudly. I scratch him under the chin.

"What do you mean you're not eating here?"

"I'm going out with Stringbean and Eric."

"Who said you could go out? Not me."

Matthew answers, "C'mon, Mom. It's Mischief Night. You don't expect me to stay home?" Mischief Night is the night before Halloween. It's when you go out and do stuff like squirt shaving cream on the windshields of parked cars and toss toilet paper into trees and shrubs and write on garage-door windows with a bar of soap.

"I don't care what night it is," says Mom. "It also happens to be a school night."

"Give me a break," Matthew replies.

"Matthew," says Mom. "You are not going out."

"I am, too. Look, Mom, I'm fourteen years old. I can do what I want."

"Oh no you can't!"

"Oh yes I can!" Matthew's voice rises in anger.

I stand up to go up to my bedroom.

"Just try and stop me," he taunts.

"Don't you talk to me like that," warns Mom.

"I'll say whatever I feel like."

I can feel my heart thumping. I wish I could smack Matthew. I do.

"I don't ever want to hear you talk that way to me again, Matthew Petruzzi," Mom says sternly. "Is that understood?"

"I hate this stupid family!" exclaims Matthew. "I really do!"

I turn, all set to rush down into the kitchen and

scream "Good! We hate you, too!" But I manage to restrain myself. Instead, I go up to my bedroom to get away from the fighting. I hate fights, period, but I especially hate it when Mom and Matthew fight. Their fights always get so vicious. I close my bedroom door and lock it. Stringbean and Eric are still playing in the attic. Stringbean is singing. His voice cracks every time he hits a high note.

I squat beside Joe's aquarium to take Joe out. I figure I'll cheer up if I play with Joe. But Joe's gone!

"Joe?" I say, looking around the room. "Where are you?" Then a horrible thought occurs to me. Oh, no, what if Mulligan got him! I leap up and start running around the room like a maniac, searching for Joe. I look for him under the bed and in the closet. I peek under the bureau, the desk, my reading chair. He's nowhere. Then I hear a small splash by the fish tank, followed by a lot of thrashing around. Joe has jumped into the fish tank, fully clothed.

"Joe!" I say, relieved, hurrying to his rescue. "What are you trying to do? Drown yourself?" I put him on top of my desk. I first help him take off his sopping wet clothes, and then I dry him off with a Kleenex. I get the hair drier from Mom's bedroom and, setting the dial on HIGH, blow hot air onto his clothes to dry them. As I am helping Joe put his clothes back on, he keeps trying to get away so he can go over and examine the hair drier, which I've

44

laid down on top of my dictionary. The minute I let go of him, he hurries over to it.

"It's a hair drier," I say. "Can you say hair drier?"

Joe doesn't say a thing.

I try again. "Haaaair driiiier."

Joe merely looks puzzled. He turns and walks over to a pencil. He picks it up.

"And that's called a pencil," I tell him. "Can you say pen-cil?"

Joe rolls his eyes and sticks the pencil into the pencil sharpener.

Suddenly, I hear Matthew storm past my bedroom door and rush up the attic stairs. The music abruptly stops. Then I hear a bunch of feet stomp down the attic stairs and go into Matthew's bedroom. Quietly, I steal over to my door and, opening it a crack, peek out. Matthew stalks past, with Stringbean and Eric

right behind him. They have their coats on. I place Joe back in his aquarium, and then I cover the aquarium with the screen that fits over it. Downstairs, the front door slams. The house is now very, very still.

It gives me this terrible, sickening feeling in the pit of my stomach.

10.

WHEN I ENTER the kitchen, Mom is at the refrigerator, with the door open. She is gazing into the freezer section. As she turns away, I see her face. She is crying. It makes *me* almost want to cry. Boy, do I hate Matthew.

"If I were you, Mom," I say. "I'd kick Matthew out of the house. I really would. I don't know why we have to put up with him. The big louse!"

Mom dumps a frozen block of lima beans into a pot and adds water from the faucet. She sets it on the stove and flicks on the burner. "We can't kick him out of the house," she says.

"Why not?"

"Because we can't. You know as well as I do he's part of this family."

"I know," I say, taking a seat on the stool that's by the counter. "I know that." I don't want her getting mad at *me* now. Sometimes Mom takes things out on me when she's really mad at Matthew. "But just because he's part of the family doesn't give him the right to be so mean. I tell you, if it were up to me, I'd kick Matthew out in a second. Then we'd be rid of him. Matthew is a big jerk! I hate him!"

Mom is wiping her eyes with the palms of her hands. She's pretty much stopped crying. "Nicole," she says. "You don't hate your brother."

"Oh, yes, I do," I declare. "Believe me, with Matthew it's not hard. You know what he did to me this afternoon? He threw me down on the floor and sat on me and wouldn't let me up."

"Well, he shouldn't have done that," is all Mom says.

"But he did!"

Mom, crossing her arms, is silent for a moment. It's so quiet, you can hear the soft, steady hum of the electric clock that's on the wall above the sink. "Matthew is going through a very difficult period in his life," Mom says, at last. "A lot of teenagers go through this period. With Matthew, it's much worse because your father and I are divorced."

Whenever Mom talks like that, I wonder what things would be like if she and Dad were still married. The thing is, even when they were married, they were constantly getting into big fights. I hated it. Boy, I tell you, when I'm a parent, I'm never going to fight. It only messes a kid up. Take Matthew. He never used to be so mean until Mom and

48

Dad started having fights all the time. "What about me?" I demand. "I'm going through a difficult period, too."

Mom comes over and, placing her hand on my back, draws me close. "I know you are, honey," she says in a low, soothing voice. "And I'm sorry. I'm proud of you. You've been managing so well, I forget how rough it is for you."

I shrug and move so we're not so close. I feel embarrassed. It's not like I'm a little kid who needs comforting. "Well, it's up to you," I say. "But I tell you, I'd sure do something about Matthew."

Mom steps over to the silverware drawer and pulls it out. "How would you like to set the table?" she asks as she takes forks, spoons, and knives from the drawer.

"Sure," I say.

Just then, there is a loud hiss from the living-room. A second later, Mulligan comes tearing into the kitchen. The little bell around his neck jingles wildly as he flies past us and disappears into the dining-room.

"What's wrong with Mulligan?" asks Mom. She turns to go into the living-room, when she nearly trips.

"Jeepers!" she cries in alarm. She places her hand on her chest and sighs. "I almost stepped on Joe!"

"Joe?" I say, astonished. I look down and, sure enough, there he is. He's gazing inquisitively about the kitchen, perfectly oblivious to the fact that he not only scared the wits out of Mulligan, but he very nearly caused Mom to trip and break her neck.

11.

"JOE, WHAT ARE YOU doing here?" I say as I reach down to pick him up. I glance at Mom. "Well, I guess we don't have to worry about Mulligan attacking Joe."

"Nicole, you shouldn't let Joe run around the house like that," says Mom irritably. She is sore because Joe startled her. She hates being startled. One time when it was getting dark, Mom was turning on the lights in the living room and I leaped out from behind a chair and cried, "Boo!" Boy, did she yell at me. I never did *that* again.

"I wasn't letting Joe run around the house," I tell her. "He escaped from his aquarium."

"What if something horrible were to happen to him while he was roaming around? You'd never forgive yourself."

"I told you, Mom, he escaped from his aquarium."

"Well, just make sure it doesn't happen again," she warns me.

"*Okay!* Gee whiz!"

Mom leans forward to address Joe. Her nose is just inches from Joe's nose. "And you, young man, are not to escape from your aquarium, you understand?" she says to Joe, but in a much, much gentler voice than the one she used in speaking to me. Mom touches the tip of her finger to Joe's nose. "You're such a cutie!" she says in this extremely nauseating, mushy voice. "Yes, you are!"

Joe rolls his eyes and Mom laughs.

"Maybe Joe would like to join us for dinner," Mom suggests.

"He'd love to!" I answer eagerly.

It dawns on me as I am setting a place for Joe at the kitchen table that he'll never be able to eat with the fork I've given him: It's almost as long as he is. Then I get this brilliant idea. I run upstairs to Mom's bedroom, take down the box of old doll furniture that's in her closet, and pull out a doll fork, spoon, knife, plate, glass, teacup and saucer. I also pull out a doll's small drop-leaf table and one of the chairs that goes with it. I bring everything downstairs to the kitchen, where I put the table and chair on top of the kitchen table. Then I wash the eating utensils in soapy water because who knows when they were cleaned last.

"Nicole, you don't know where the big frying pan

is, do you?" asks Mom, as she is unstacking the dish-washer.

"The big frying pan?" I say as the phone rings.

Mom walks over and picks it up. "Hello? Oh, hi Fran." It's Marcia's mother. "No, it's true," Mom says into the receiver. "It's really alive. Apparently, they found him up in the attic—God knows how, that attic is such a mess. From what I gather, Nicole gave the doll some sort of formula she created from an old chemistry set."

While Mom is talking, I scoot upstairs, get the frying pan and the broom from the attic, and pick up the food from my bedroom. When I return to the kitchen, Mom is still on the phone. "Well, I don't know what we're going to do with him, really. But please don't tell anyone about him. The last thing I need is to have a lot of people calling up to find out if it's really true. Anyway, wait till you see him. He's the cutest thing."

As I sort of suspected, during dinner Mom brings up the subject of what we're going to do with Joe.

"Who'd we give him to?" I demand in a hostile voice.

Mom shrugs. "Well, maybe a university or a labo-ratory. Some place where he could be studied. It isn't every day a G.I. Joe doll comes to life."

I look at Joe. He is seated at his little table, hap-pily eating one of the Goldfish crackers I put on his plate. He holds the cracker in both hands like a squirrel would. "If it hadn't been for me, he wouldn't be alive," I remind her.

"I realize that, Nicole. But I have a hunch that taking care of Joe won't be as easy as you think it will be."

"I know it won't be easy," I reply.

"Do you?" asks Mom. "It means a big responsibility. You'll always have to be thinking of Joe as well as yourself. For instance, you'll have to dress him and bathe him and feed him—and I don't mean letting him eat snacks all day long."

"He won't," I vow in a determined voice.

"And what if Joe doesn't behave the way you'd like him to? What will you do?"

"That won't happen," I say.

"Oh no? And what if he gets on your nerves the way your brother does? Will you want to kick *him* out of the house, too?"

"Of course not!" I answer. "I don't think that's fair—comparing Joe to Matthew."

"You don't?"

"No." Suddenly I get this idea how I might be able to get Mom to let me keep Joe. "I feel just like you felt when you got that little bunny rabbit," I say.

Mom's eyes are fixed on Joe. She looks at me. "Nicole," she says. "There's a big difference between a little bunny rabbit and a living, breathing G.I. Joe doll."

54

"Tell me the story about the bunny rabbit," I say.

Mom winces. "You don't want to hear that old story *again.*"

"Yes, I do," I say, although Mom has told it so often I know the story by heart. "Honest."

Mom hesitates. I nod. "Well," she begins with a shrug. "A boy who lived down the road from us and who was a friend of your Uncle Greg's was giving away these bunny rabbits. Now I happened to love rabbits. I took one and brought it home and kept it in my bedroom without telling anybody. I was afraid that if my father—your grandfather—found out I had a rabbit, he'd make me get rid of it."

"How mean!" I cry.

"Little did I know, though, that the bunny would leave its droppings all over my bedroom carpet."

"You're kidding me!" I exclaim. I hope Mom isn't going to drag out this story. I've just remembered that my favorite game show, "Wheel of Fortune," is on.

"Oh, you should've *heard* your grandfather when he found out about that rabbit. You never heard anyone rant and rave so much in all your life," she says, laughing, as she lifts her glass of wine. Mom always laughs at this point in the story.

I laugh, too. "So what happened then?" I ask, glancing at the clock above the sink.

"Well, after your grandfather calmed down, we vacuumed and shampooed my bedroom carpet."

"But what happened about the bunny rabbit?"

"He helped me build a rabbit hutch in the back-yard."

I open my eyes wide. "You mean, Grandpa let you keep him? Boy, that sure was nice of him!"

Mom gives me a suspicious look. I shrug. Mom laughs. "Okay," she says. "You win. You can keep Joe—at least for the time being."

I turn to Joe. "Hear that, Joe? I can keep you!" He is nibbling on a lima bean, but I can tell by the horrible face he is making that he doesn't like it. "Thanks, Mom," I say. "Don't worry. I'll take good care of him. I really will."

12.

ACTING LIKE I just remembered, I cry, "Hey, we're missing 'Wheel of Fortune'!" I reach over and turn on the small TV set that's on a stand beside the kitchen table.

A dorky-looking guy in glasses is spinning the huge wheel. He claps his hands, shouting, "C'mon, a thousand dollars!" The wheel stops at $350.

"What letter will it be?" asks the gameshow host.

"Are there any N's?" asks the man.

"Yes, there are two N's," says the gameshow host.

The board shows __ __w y__ __'re __ __lk__ __g. It's a phrase.

Mom gets it immediately. "Now you're talking!" she says triumphantly, as the N's are being flipped over.

Actually, I could have answered it if Mom hadn't. That's because it's a phrase Dad used to say. "Now you're talking!" he always said whenever Matthew or I suggested something he thought was a really terrific idea—like getting ice-cream cones on a boiling hot day or playing wiffle ball out in the backyard after he got home from work on a summer evening. I miss those days. I miss Dad. He lives in Los Angeles with his new wife, Liz. During summer vacation, I go out and spend a few weeks with them. We always do fun things, like visit Disneyland and go to the beach. Dad always asks me about a hundred million questions about Matthew. He always wants to know how he's doing and if he still has his rock-and-roll band.

Matthew never goes out to see Dad. Matthew won't even talk to him over the phone. He hates Dad. He hates Dad for getting a divorce from Mom and marrying Liz. He said so himself. I used to be mad at Dad, too, but I'm not anymore. Last summer when I was out visiting Dad, we talked about the divorce and Dad told me that one of the worst things for him was having Matthew so angry at him. He said he hoped that maybe one day he and Matthew could be friends. I didn't want to hurt Dad's feelings, but I wanted to tell him that I wouldn't hold my breath, if I were him.

"I'd like to buy a vowel," says the man. "I'd like to buy an O."

"Let's see," says the gameshow host. "There are two O's."

The man studies the puzzle, then says, "I'll spin again." He leans over and gives the wheel a good spin. "C'mon! C'mon!" he shouts, clapping. The wheel slows down. It passes $750, crawls past $500, then stops. Bankrupt. The man, groaning, slaps his forehead in disappointment.

Joe is in a trance, watching the TV. He slaps *his* forehead.

Mom says, "I want you to eat all your lima beans, Nicole."

I grimace. "Do I have to?"

"Yes, you have to," she says. "Look at Joe's plate. He ate all *his* lima beans."

I look, but I don't believe it. He doesn't have a single lima bean left. And *I* thought he hated them. I'm tempted to give him mine, since he likes them so much, but Mom would only get upset. I force myself to eat my lima beans. I figure if Joe can eat them, so can I.

"Do you want to spin again or would you like to answer the puzzle?" the gameshow host is asking another contestant, a fat woman named Phyllis.

"I'll solve the puzzle," says Phyllis with a big, goofy smile. "Now you're talking."

"That's it!" cries the gameshow host.

"Took you long enough," Mom says to the TV as she gets up from the kitchen table. She takes her plate, Joe's tiny plate, and my plate to the sink.

"Now weren't those lima beans just yummy?" she asks me.

"No," I answer.

On her way back to the table, Mom stops and exclaims, "Oh, Nicole!" in a disapproving voice.

"What?"

She points to a spot under the table by my chair. Lima beans are scattered all over the rug. So *that's* what happened to Joe's lima beans! "I'm not the least bit amused," says Mom, who thinks *I* put them there.

I want to tell Mom who the lima beans really belong to, but I can't. Not after her big lecture on how difficult it's going to be to take care of Joe.

"Now I want you to clean up every one of those lima beans," Mom orders.

While I am getting out the whisk broom and dustpan, the phone rings. "I've got it," I say, and pick up the phone.

It's Marcia. "I just had this really cool idea," she says excitedly. "Let's bring Joe to school with us tomorrow."

"I was just going to call you and say the exact same thing," I lie to her. I don't want Marcia to know that she thought of something I didn't. Especially something I wish I had thought of first.

"You're kidding me!" exclaims Marcia. "I guess great minds think alike."

"I guess so," I say.

13.

AFTER I HANG UP the phone, I clean up the lima beans and then, collecting Joe, I excuse myself from the table.

"No mocha-chip ice cream?" asks Mom.

I shake my head. "I'm full." I pat my stomach.

"Have you done all your homework?"

"I just have to finish my report on Madame Curie."

"I don't want you playing with Joe until you've done all your homework," Mom says. "Remember what I said about responsibility."

"Yes," I sigh. I can tell I'm going to be hearing a lot about this responsibility business from here on out.

Up in my bedroom, I can't seem to concentrate on the book about Madame Curie that I took out from the library. That's because Joe is in the corner of my desk, sharpening pencils, and the noise of the pencil sharpener is driving me up a wall.

It takes me long enough, but I finally write my report. I write that Madame Curie, who was born in 1867, was the daughter of teachers in Poland. She came to Paris, France, to study physics and chemistry. In 1895, she married Pierre Curie. Together they discovered that uranium ore contains two highly radioactive chemical elements: radium and polonium. This earned them the 1903 Nobel Prize in physics. Madame Curie received another Nobel Prize in 1911, this time in chemistry. She got it for all the work she was doing on radium and polonium. Radium and polonium are important to us because we use them to make nuclear bombs, among other things. Madame Curie died in 1934, of leukemia.

Sitting back, I check my report for any misspelled words. I made sure to write in large, slanting letters so my report looks longer than it really is. Basically, I wrote down what was written on Madame Curie in the encyclopedia. I just changed a word here and there so Mrs. Babcock, my science teacher, can't say I copied it. She's always accusing someone in the class of copying. Only she calls it plagiarism. I decide to change the word *leukemia,* a word I just know will make Mrs. Babcock suspicious. I look up the word in my dictionary. Then I erase *leukemia* and write *cancer.* If I were really being honest, I'd also write down that I wish dumb old Madame Curie hadn't discovered radium or polonium. Then we wouldn't have to worry about countries getting into a big war and using nuclear bombs that could destroy the entire world. But I suppose if Madame Curie hadn't discovered radium or polonium, somebody else would have.

I put my report into my knapsack, and then I go to my closet to figure out what I am going to wear to school tomorrow. I pull out my black-and-white tartan skirt and my white turtleneck. I am gazing into my closet trying to make up my mind whether to wear my red sweater or my orange sweater when, behind me, I hear a tiny voice say "I'd like to buy a valve."

I freeze.

"I'd like to buy a valve," the little voice says again.

I spin around. Joe is standing on my desk, holding a pencil stub.

"I'd like to buy a valve," he says, looking up at me.

I practically trip over myself as I rush out of my bedroom. "Hey, Mom! *Mom!*" I holler at the top of my lungs. "Get up here, quick!"

Mom hurries out of the kitchen, carrying a magazine in her hand. "What is it?" she asks, worriedly, as she starts up the back stairs.

"It's Joe," I say. "You won't believe this, but he talks!"

14.

"HE TALKS?" Mom says as she enters my bedroom. She stops before the desk to observe Joe.

"Listen," I say.

We wait, our eyes glued to Joe, but he doesn't even make so much as a peep.

"Wouldn't you know it?" I say to Mom, feeling rather embarrassed. "Now he's not talking." I sit down at my desk. "Joe," I say, in a firm voice. "Talk!"

"Say something, Joe," says Mom, after a few moments.

"I said, talk!" I order him.

"Let's hear you talk, Joe," Mom coaxes.

"Joe," I say, growing impatient. "Will you *talk*!"

But does he? No. He cocks his head. He rolls his eyes. He slaps his forehead.

Mom, smiling, says, "That's good, Joe." She turns to me, asking, "What did he say?"

"I'd like to buy a vowel. Only he said *valve.*"

Mom thinks I'm joking. "He didn't say that."

"He *did*!" I exclaim, pushing my chair back and standing. "I know it sounds dumb, but he did. Really." I turn to Joe. "Why won't you talk?"

"Well, if he talks again, give me a holler."

"I wish he'd talk for you," I say as I follow Mom to the door. "He really did talk. He did—really."

Suddenly Joe blurts out "I'd like to buy a valve. An O."

I turn around, crying "That-a-boy!"

Mom mutters, "I don't believe it. This is crazy."

I pat Joe on the head. I'm so proud of him. "What a good boy!"

"What did you say was in that formula you gave him?" asks Mom.

"I told you. I just mixed some chemicals that were in Matthew's old Mr. Chemistry set with some stuff from the second floor bathroom."

"Do you still have the formula?"

I shake my head. "I flushed it down the toilet."

"Jeepers," exclaims Mom, marveling at Joe. "This is incredible."

"I'll be right back," I say. "I have to tell Marcia."

I run into Mom's bedroom and call Marcia, but her phone is busy. It's probably her older brother, Adam, who's on the phone. He's *always* on the phone talking to his girlfriend. I try three times before I finally give up in frustration and return to my bedroom. Seated at my desk, Mom is holding up a golf tee that she got from the top drawer of my desk.

"Can you say golf tee?" she asks Joe.

Joe stares at her with a blank face.

I come over and stand beside Mom. "Has he said anything else?"

"Uh-uh," says Mom as, rising, she hands me the golf tee. "He just keeps saying, 'I'd like to buy a valve.'"

15.

AFTER MOM GOES, I try teaching Joe new words. I hold up the hand mirror that I keep on top of my bureau. "This is a mirror, Joe," I say. "Can you say *mirror*?"

Joe is fascinated by his reflection. He touches the scar on his cheek.

"That's you!" I say.

Joe reaches out to grab the mirror, but I pull it away. "When you want something, there's a word you have to say, and that word is *please*," I explain to him, but I can tell he doesn't understand.

"Please," I say again.

"Pleee," says Joe.

I clap my hands. "That's it!" I say. "Now just add *zzz*. Pleeze."

"Pleee," says Joe.

"Pleeze," I correct him.

68

"Pleeeze," he says.

"Good boy!" I exclaim. I pat him on the head and point to the mirror. "This is a mirror. Now you say it. Mirror."

Joe gapes at himself in the mirror.

"You can say it. Mirror."

"Miwwa," says Joe as he steps closer to the mirror.

"Mirror."

"Miwwa."

"Mirror."

"Mirwa."

"Good enough!" I say, in a very approving voice.

Joe touches the scar on the side of his face again.

"Scar," I say.

"Scar," he says.

I get up and open my jewelry box. A little plastic ballerina pops up and starts to slowly spin a pirouette as the jewelry box plays "Edelweiss." I take out a Band-Aid, unwrap it, and peel off the paper strip that's on the back of the sticky part.

"Band-Aid," I say to Joe as I'm about to place it over his scar.

"Band-Aid," he says.

The only problem is, the Band-Aid is too big for his face.

"Oh, well," I say and toss it into the wastebasket. "Oh, wastebasket," I explain, tapping the wastebasket.

"Oh, wastebasket," says Joe.

I go around the room, pointing and picking up things and telling Joe what they are. "Bookcase. Books. Photographs. Walkman. Marble. Miniature horses. Bureau. Lamp. Jewelry box. Ballerina. Ring. Watch. Barrette. Comb. Bed. Closet. Dresses. Coat hanger. Desk. Eraser. Rubber band. Pencils. Pencil sharpener. Golf tee."

Joe points to the framed photograph of Mom and me that is on my bookcase. Matthew took the picture last Christmas. I take it down to show Joe. He points to Mom.

"That's Mom," I say. I point to me. "And that's me."

Joe points to me in the photograph and says, "Me."

"No, that's not you, that's me," I say.

Joe looks lost.

I point to myself. "I'm Nicole. *Nicole.*"

"Neeco," says Joe.

I shake my head. "Ni-cole," I say very slowly and deliberately.

"Nee-co," says Joe just as slowly and deliberately as I said it. He points to Mom in the picture. "Mom."

"No, that's *my* Mom," I say. "You should call her Mrs. Petruzzi."

"Mizziz Peetrooozi," says Joe in a hesitant voice.

I nod vigorously. "That's right!"

"Mizziz Peetrooozi," Joe says, much more confidently now. He points to me. "Neeco."

"No, *Nicole!*"

"Neeco."

"Tell you what," I say. "Since you're having so much trouble saying it, and since in a way I am sort of your mother, why don't you just call me mommy." I point to myself. "Mommy."

"Mommy," says Joe without any trouble. Turning, he points to another photograph on my bookcase.

"That's Matthew," I say, taking the photograph down. It's a photograph that Dad took a long time ago. It shows Matthew sitting on the front steps of our house. He has a really bad haircut. It's one of the few pictures that exists where he's smiling. He really does have a nice smile. It's too bad he doesn't smile more often.

"Matthew," says Joe.

"He's a big jerk," I say.

"He's a big jerk," repeats Joe.

I go to my desk and take my wallet out from one of the drawers, and from my wallet I take out a snapshot of Marcia. "Marcia," I say.

Joe smiles. He knows who *she* is. "*Marcia!*" he says. He points to the hat Marcia is wearing. He looks mystified.

"Oh, that's a *hat*," I explain. "She wasn't wearing it when you saw her."

Joe says, "Hat."

"A dorky hat," I say.

"Dorky?"

"It means dumb. Stupid. It comes from the word *dork.*"

"Dork?"

"Yeah, you know: He's a real dork."

Joe looks terribly confused.

"See, some people are dorks," I tell him. "They do dorky things. Dumb things. They can't help it."

Joe points to Marcia's hat. "Dorky."

"Good boy!" I exclaim, clapping.

He points to Marcia. "Dork," he says.

I shake my head. "Wrong! Wrong! Wrong!" I say.

"That's *Marcia*. She is not a dork. I mean, sure, she may do some pretty dorky things sometimes, but she's not a dork."

Joe steps over to the photograph of Matthew. It is lying face up on the carpet. "Matthew," he says. "He-is-a-big-jerk."

"Wow, you learn fast!" I exclaim, amazed and delighted.

16.

AT TEN MINUTES to ten, Mom walks into my bedroom, announcing, "Time for bed."

"Ask Joe a question," I tell her. I am lying on my side on the floor with my hand under my head. Joe is standing in front of me. A Kleenex box, a stapler, a pad of yellow stickies, a snowman paperweight, a picture of a man that I drew to show Joe the different parts of the body, and a dispenser of Scotch tape—the things I've been teaching Joe to say—lie all about on the floor.

"Go on. Ask Joe anything."

"What's the capital of Ecuador?" asks Mom as she turns back the covers on my bed.

"Not *that* kind of question!" I say. "A *real* question. Like what's my favorite dessert."

"Now how's the little guy supposed to know something like that?"

"Just ask him."

Mom makes a face as if the whole thing is ridiculous. She shrugs. "What is Nicole's favorite dessert?"

"Joe," I say. "What is Mommy's favorite dessert?"

Joe answers "Hot apple pie with a scoop of vanilla ice cream and a glass of milk."

I burst out laughing. "Not bad, eh? Now ask him what my favorite TV show is."

"You got him to say new words!" cries Mom.

Joe bows. "It is a pleasure to meet you, Mizziz Peetrooozzi," he says—just as I instructed him to.

Mom roars with laughter. "It is a pleasure to meet you, too, Joe."

I puff on my stubby fingernails and brush them back and forth across the front of my sweater. "I taught him everything he knows."

"Then you must be tired as anything," says Mom.

"No, I'm not," I protest.

Mom is studying Joe. "I don't think Joe should stay in your bedroom tonight," she says.

I jump to my feet. "Why not?"

"Because I don't think it's such a good idea."

"Why?"

"Because I don't," she answers. "He can sleep in the attic. Actually, it's too messy up there. He can sleep in the guest room. You can leave the door open, and I'll put the cat in the laundry room."

"Why can't he stay in my room? That's so stupid!"

I say and sit down on the edge of my bed. I kick off my sneakers.

"Maybe so," says Mom, giving me a good-night kiss. "But those are the rules."

"What do you think? He's going to murder me in my sleep?" I ask, but I can see there's no point in arguing. Mom leaves and I slip into my blue flannel nightgown. Then I tuck Joe into his little bed. I stick the pencil sharpener and some pencils into the aquarium. That's so Joe can have something to do in

case he can't fall asleep right away. I place the screen over the top, and tape it down with Scotch tape. I lift up the aquarium and lug it, with the cord to the pencil sharpener dragging along the floor, down the hallway and into the guest room. I set it down on the floor and plug the pencil sharpener into a wall outlet. Then I crouch down and peer in at Joe through the screen mesh.

"Well, good night, Joe."

"Good night, Mommy," he says.

He looks so adorable all curled up, with his hands tucked under his head. I turn off the light and leave the door open a small crack so that light from the hallway will shine in.

I lay down in bed, but I'm so hyper, I have trouble falling asleep. I stare at the ceiling, thinking. I'm thinking that I really should patent this formula I made today. Then I could go into business selling the stuff. Little girls all over the world would buy it to give to their dolls. I'd be a millionaire, three, maybe four times over by the time I turn fifteen. Why, I might even win a Nobel Prize in chemistry. The only thing is, I'm not sure I can remember exactly how much of each ingredient I put in.

Then I hear Mom's and Matthew's voices coming from the heating duct in my wall. They are talking in such low, serious voices, I really have to strain to hear what they are saying.

"I'm sorry I lost my temper," says Mom.

"It's no big deal," says Matthew.

"Well, I'm sorry."

I can't believe Mom is actually apologizing to Matthew. I really can't. She *always* apologizes to him after they have a big fight, even when Matthew started it. I'm annoyed at Mom for giving in to Matthew. I am. One time I asked Mom why she let Matthew get away with murder, and Mom replied that she didn't, really.

"Then how come you're always forgiving him?"

"Nicole," she said. "I know Matthew may not always be easy to be around, but he does have a nice side to him."

"Yeah, right!" I said.

While I am lying there, thinking these things, the headlights of a car appear on the wall above my bureau. They slide across the wall and slip onto the next wall and then they disappear, leaving me in darkness.

17.

I'M AWAKENED VERY early the next morning by the steady whine of an electric pencil sharpener. It is still quite dark in my bedroom. The clock on my radio says 6:05.

I rise, put on my bathrobe, and go out into the hallway. Mom is up. There is a light under her bedroom door and her radio is on, tuned to an all-news station. I enter the guest room and flick on the light switch. Joe is up and at his pencil sharpener—he's already sharpened six pencils into tiny stubs.

"My, you're up early," I say.

"It is a pleasure to meet you!" Joe cries cheerfully, above the whir of the pencil sharpener.

I take Joe into the bathroom with me so he can wash up. He's fascinated by the faucets.

"This is the hot water faucet and this is the cold water faucet," I explain, turning each one on.

Joe sticks his hand into the stream of cold water.

"Brrr!" I say, shivering. "Cold!"

"Brrr!" Joe says, shivering. "Cold!"

Mom is standing at the kitchen table serving oatmeal when Joe and I come down for breakfast. She's wearing an apron so she won't spill anything on the green dress she is wearing to work.

"Better give Joe an extra big helping," I say as I set Joe down at his little table. I sit down at my place and pick up my spoon. "He's got a big day in store for him."

"What do you mean?" Mom asks.

"I'm taking Joe to school with me," I say.

"Oh no you're not!" says Mom, putting the pot down in the sink. She carries the lid to the pot back to the kitchen table and places it over Matthew's bowl to keep his oatmeal warm.

"Why can't I?"

"Because I don't want you to," says Mom, sitting down in her chair.

"Why?"

"Because I don't."

"But why?"

"Nicole, if I have to explain myself every time I don't want you to do something with Joe, I'll think twice about letting you keep him."

"This isn't fair!" I announce, and mush my oatmeal around in my bowl.

"Stop pouting."

"I'm not pouting. It's just that I don't want to leave Joe in the house all day by himself."

"I said no, Nicole," says Mom in a no-uncertain-terms voice. "Joe will be perfectly fine in his aquarium until you get home from school."

"What are you talking about?" asks Matthew, who's just walked into the kitchen. He's been in the shower. His hair, wet and combed, is slicked to one side of his head.

"Good morning, Matthew," says Mom pleasantly. She leans across the table and takes the lid off his bowl. Steam rises up. "Does Matthew know about Joe?" Mom asks me.

"Joe who?" asks Matthew, taking a seat. "Oh, *that* Joe. Yeah, we met." He looks at me. "Hey, thanks a lot for letting me show him to Stringbean and Eric."

I make a face at Matthew.

Joe waves to Matthew. Matthew nearly spits out the orange juice he's just sipped.

Joe rolls his eyes and then slaps his forehead.

"I love it!" cries Matthew, laughing, drumming his fingers on the table. "Awesome! Totally awesome!"

I can see by the happy look on Joe's face that he loves being the center of attention. He points to Matthew, saying, "Matthew!"

"Hey, the little dude talks!" Matthew says.

Joe repeats, "Matthew!"

"He must think pretty highly of me to keep saying my name," Matthew says.

"Yeah, right!" I reply grumpily.

"Matthew!" Joe says again.

"Hey, dude!" Matthew says. Then he turns to me and says, "Pass the milk, will you?"

"When you want something, there's a word you have to say," says Joe. "And that word is pleeezze!"

Matthew and Mom howl with laughter. Angry as I am, even I laugh—only not as hard.

"Could you pass the milk—pleeeze!" says Matthew. "By the way, did anyone hear a strange noise last night?"

"What kind of a noise?" asks Mom.

Matthew shrugs. "I'm not sure."

"I didn't hear anything," Mom says.

"Maybe I dreamt it," he says. "Boy, I had the worst nightmare last night."

"What happened?"

"It was really horrible. I dreamt I was in the dentist's chair and the dentist was drilling every last one of my teeth. *Vrrr! Vrrr! Vrrr!*"

"Matthew," says Joe.

"Yeah, dude?"

"You're a big jerk!"

Matthew looks as if someone slapped him across the face. The thing is, I can tell by the innocent look on Joe's face that he thinks he's just paid Matthew a big compliment. I quickly grab Joe, saying, "Well, time to put Joe back into his aquarium so I can get ready for school."

I carry Joe upstairs, but I don't put him into his aquarium. I zip him up in the outside pocket of my blue knapsack so I can take him to school without Mom seeing him. I know I am being dishonest and going against Mom's orders, but I don't think it's fair that she won't let me take Joe to school when she knows it means so much to me. Before heading downstairs, I go into the guest room and place the screen on top of the aquarium. I deliberately put it on crooked. That's so if Mom looks in on Joe before she leaves, she'll think he escaped from his aquarium. She won't have time to look for him because she'll be late for work. I close the guest room door. That's so she'll think he's hiding in the guest room. I don't want her worrying all day that Joe is wandering around the house turning on stove burners or toppling over lamps.

18.

I MEET MARCIA, as usual, at the end of my street. She is standing on the sidewalk near a street sign that looks as if it has been gift wrapped with toilet paper—the work of some kids roaming around on Mischief Night. The trees that line the street are all different colors—bright red, gold, greenish yellow— and piles of leaves are lying along the edge of the street. Marcia is bundled up in her red parka, a scarf, and that dumb hat she always wears. It is a cloudy, cold autumn morning. You can see your breath.

"Where's Joe?" asks Marcia.

I unsling my knapsack and unzip the outside pocket. "Right here," I say as Joe pops his head up.

"Well, look who's here!" says Marcia gaily.

I put my knapsack around my right shoulder so I can see Joe, and then we start to walk along the sidewalk, past a house with a smiling pumpkin on its front doorstep.

"How did Joe sleep last night?" asks Marcia.

"Why don't you ask him?" I say.

Marcia scrunches up her nose. "Ask him?"

"Sure."

"Cut it out."

"Cut what out?" I say. "Okay. I'll ask him. How did you sleep last night, Joe?"

"How did I do what?" he asks.

Marcia shrieks with delight. "Geez Louise! He can talk now?"

"Pretty neat, huh?" I say.

She gives me a suspicious look. "You're not doing ventriloquism, are you?"

I laugh. "No, I'm not doing ventriloquism."

"How does he know how to talk?"

85

"How do you think? I taught him. I spent all last night teaching him words. Joe is getting better and better at conversation all the time. Aren't you, Joe?"

"Yes, Mommy," says Joe.

"*Mommy!*" exclaims Marcia.

I shrug. "Well, I am sort of his mommy."

"What does that make me?" asks Marcia. "His *daddy?*"

"Brrr!" says Joe, shivering, folding his arms. "Cold!"

"Look at Joe!" cries Marcia. "He's shivering! And no wonder! He's only wearing his fatigues! Nicole, you shouldn't let Joe go out in this weather without a coat!"

"I was in such a rush, I forgot," I say as I set my knapsack down on the sidewalk and pull off my scarf. I wrap the scarf around Joe's body, leaving his arms free to move around. I put Joe back into the pocket of the knapsack, and we continue on our way.

Joe points to Marcia's hat. "You are wearing your hat."

"Why, yes I am," she says, clearly pleased, touching it.

"It looks dorky," says Joe, hoping to please Marcia still more.

Marcia stops and looks at Joe. "It looks *dorky?*"

Oh, brother, I groan to myself. I quickly try to explain. "He doesn't mean—"

"Marcia is a real dork!" cries Joe happily.

"A *dork*!" exclaims Marcia.

"Now, Joe, that's not what I taught you," I say to him.

Marcia gives me a fierce look. "Just what *did* you teach him?"

"Nothing," I reply, putting the collar of my turtleneck up. My neck feels cold without a scarf. "I just told him you wear a dorky hat."

"I'll have you know my grandmother made me this hat," Marcia says.

"I know. But Marcia, face it. It's a dorky-looking hat."

"It is not!"

"It is too! I wouldn't be caught dead wearing it."

"Well! This *is* revealing! *That's* why you're always telling me it's not cold enough to wear a hat."

"It is not," I lie.

"Now I know the truth! You're just embarrassed to be seen with me when I have my hat on."

"Marcia, that's not so and you know it."

Marcia pulls off her hat. "There!" she cries, stuffing the hat into her coat pocket. "I'm not wearing it anymore. I hope you're happy. And don't worry, Nicole, if I come down with pneumonia because I'm not wearing my hat—excuse me, my *dorky* hat—I won't tell a soul that it was because of you."

I heave a huge sigh and look down at Joe. He's so

upset by our fight, his bottom lip is sticking out. I feel just rotten. What am I doing, anyway, quarreling over a dorky hat? Boy, I wish I knew how I get myself into these things.

19.

FOR ALMOST THE ENTIRE walk to school, Marcia doesn't say a word to me. Not one word. But then, hearing the yells and screams of kids playing way off in the direction of our school, she says, in this excited voice, "I can't wait to see everyone's faces when they see Joe."

That's what I like about Marcia—she never stays mad for very long. Some kids—and even grown-ups, for that matter—get mad and stay mad and won't talk to you for days and days. But not Marcia.

"Me too," I say.

"Hey, maybe they'll call an assembly so we can show Joe to the entire school. We'll be celebrities!"

A horrifying thought occurs to me. "Wait a sec!" I say and stop. "We can't show Joe to anybody!"

Marcia stops. She looks surprised. "Why not?"

"I wasn't supposed to bring Joe to school. If my mom hears that I brought Joe to school, she'll kill me."

"Uh-oh!" says Marcia.

"Uh-oh!" says Joe.

"Think I should run home real quick and put him in his aquarium?" I ask.

"Uh-oh!" says Joe again.

"You'll be late for school," Marcia says.

"What'll I do?" I ask, panicking.

"Uh-oh!" Joe says once again.

"We can always keep Joe in my locker," offers Marcia.

"Uh-oh!" says Joe *again*.

"Or mine," I say, and we start walking again.

"Why don't we ask Joe which locker he'd prefer to stay in," suggests Marcia.

"That's the dumbest thing I've heard in a long time."

"What's so dumb about it?"

"Uh-oh!" says Joe.

"What does Joe know about lockers?"

"Well, it doesn't hurt to ask." She leans forward and cranes her neck to put her face right up close to Joe's face. "Hey, Joe. Whose locker would you rather stay in today? Mine or Nicole's? I just cleaned mine two days ago, by the way."

"Uh-oh!" says Joe.

"Now before you decide, let me show you what I

have in my locker." She unzips her knapsack and pulls out a Ring Ding from her lunch bag.

"I don't want Joe filling up on snacks all day long," I inform Marcia. "From now on, he's going to have a well-balanced diet."

Marcia looks at me in disbelief. "What are you? The school nurse?"

"Uh-oh!" says Joe.

"Look, Marcia, here's what we'll do," I say. "We'll keep Joe in my locker, and I'll owe you a favor. I'll just feel tons easier if he's in my locker."

"He'll be safe in my locker, too," she insists as we start to walk past Tommy Tarentino's house. Whenever we pass Tommy Tarentino's house, Marcia slows down and looks at the gray-shingled house with white trim. She has a huge crush on Tommy Tarentino.

"I know he will," I say. "But it's hard to explain. I'll just feel much better if he's in my locker."

Marcia thinks this over. "Okay," she finally says, and unzips her knapsack to put the Ring Ding back into her lunch bag.

"Oh, no, my sandwich is getting squished!" she cries. She takes out some notebook papers that are held together by a big paperclip, sets them down on the sidewalk, and fixes her lunch bag. Marcia is about to put the bag and the notebook papers back into her knapsack when I notice that the top page, which is covered with Marcia's handwriting, begins: Dear Friend.

"What's this?" I ask, pulling off the top sheet.

Marcia snatches it from my hand. "Nothing."

"It's the chain letter, isn't it?"

"Uh-oh!" says Joe.

Marcia doesn't answer. She stuffs the paper back into her knapsack and zips the knapsack up.

"Admit it. That's what it is."

"All right, I admit it," she says. "It's the chain letter."

"I thought I told you to ignore it."

"Sure," replies Marcia. "And get roughed up by six racketeers. Hey, no thanks."

"Well, you'd better not send me one," I warn her. "Actually, you know what I'd do if I were you?"

"What?"

"I'd send letters to kids I thought really deserved them. You know, someone like Joanna Binkley. She's a big tub of lard who thinks she knows everything."

"Uh-oh!" says Joe.

We turn the corner. Just down the street is our school. It's an old brick building with tall, many-paned windows. You can tell which rooms the first, second, and third graders are in: the ones with the windows decorated with pumpkins, witches, and black cats. Kids wearing mittens and winter coats are lining up in the school yard to file into the building.

To make sure nobody sees Joe, I push his head down and zip up the outside pocket of my knapsack.

We enter the building and go straight to my locker. My locker is so full of junk that my baseball glove falls out when I open the locker door.

"What a mess!" remarks Marcia disapprovingly, as she peers over my shoulder.

Ignoring her, I glance about the corridor to make sure nobody is looking. I take Joe out of my knapsack and put him into my locker, setting him down on top of the mountain of books and loose papers and spiral notebooks and pencils and pens and my white sweatshirt and Mom's folding umbrella and my running shoes. I unzip the other part of my knapsack and pull out a couple of books and my science report on Madame Curie. I put them into my locker. "Now don't worry, Joe," I say, taking my English book from the locker. "I'll be back in a little bit."

"Uh-oh!" is all Joe says.

20.

ALL DURING ENGLISH, I keep asking myself: Why did I ever bring Joe to school? I'm so worried about him all alone in my dark locker. He's probably terrified, the poor little guy. Why didn't I just listen to Mom and leave him at home? The minute the class ends, I go check on Joe. I am about to open my locker when I hear a "Hi, Nicole!" just behind me. I practically leap out of my shoes. It's Monica Quigley and Dana Erickson.

"Can we see the G.I. Joe doll?" asks Monica.

With a perfectly innocent face, I say "What G.I. Joe doll?"

"The one Marcia told us about," says Dana.

I am going to kill Marcia, I say to myself. I smile and lie. "I don't know anything about a G.I. Joe doll."

Who pops up out of nowhere then but Joanna Binkley. She pushes a space for herself between Monica and Dana. She is wearing the exact same red

94

sweater I almost wore today. (Thank goodness I didn't.)

"Guess what I got?" she demands. She sounds really annoyed. "A stupid chain letter!" She holds the chain letter up, rattling it. "Grrrr! Boy, would I love to get my hands on the person who put this in my locker."

From inside my locker, two little fists pound on the locker door. Joe's small voice cries out: "Mommy!"

I want to open the locker to see what's wrong with Joe, but I don't dare, not with everyone around.

"Mommy!" Joe's voice calls out again.

Joanna Binkley stares at my locker. "What do you have in there?" she asks. "That's not a Talking Tina, is it?"

"Let me out of here, Mommy!"

I yank open my locker door. Joe, looking pale and faint, tumbles out into my hands. Monica, Dana, and Joanna Binkley all gasp at once.

Joe sways, blinks, and fans the air by his nose. One whiff inside my locker tells me what's troubling him—the smelly socks that are stuffed inside my running shoes.

Still fanning the air, Joe looks up and sees the small audience gathered before him. He instantly stands as straight as a soldier at attention. "It is a pleasure to meet you!" he announces and bows.

Joanna Binkley shrieks. Terrified, I push Joe back

in my locker and slam the door. "Would you shut up!" I snap at her.

Joanna Binkley stammers, "What—what—is—it?"

"It's a dumb G.I. Joe doll," I say, glaring at her. She looks pretty shaken up.

"But it's—it's alive!"

Dana explains, "Marcia said it has something to do with a chain letter she received."

Joanna Binkley looks at her. "Marcia got a chain letter, too?"

"Marcia doesn't know what she's talking about," I say.

"Can we see the G.I. Joe again?" asks Monica.

I hesitate.

"I promise I won't scream," says Joanna Binkley.

I make them all swear they won't tell a soul that I have Joe in my locker. They swear, and I open the locker.

Joe is on top of a notebook with his left foot wedged in between the wire spirals. He is tugging at his leg to free it. "Oh, I'm sorry, Joe," I apologize, and help him pull his foot out.

Monica gushes, "He's so cute!"

Oh, no, I think, now Joe is going to start acting cute. Which is exactly what he does. He rolls his eyes. He cocks his head. He certainly has this cuteness routine down pat.

The three girls giggle. "Ohhh!" says Dana.

Joe slaps his forehead, and they all laugh. He slaps
his forehead a couple more times.

"He's adorable!" exclaims Joanna Binkley.

Joe does something new then. "Awesome!" he

says. This really produces a big laugh. In fact, *awesome* goes over so well, he says it three more times. Then he does another new thing. "Geez Louise!" he cries—just the way Marcia would. "Geez Louise!" he says again and again. Then he does *something else* new. Mimicking my voice, he says: "Yeah, right!" He says it *very* sarcastically. I never realized how horrible it sounds. I stare at Joe, stunned and hurt.

"Perfect!" cries Joanna Binkley. "He sounds just like you, Nicole!"

I don't know whom I want to bop more—Joanna Binkley or Joe.

"So what do you think of Joe?" I hear Marcia say from behind Dana. Dana and Monica step aside to let Marcia in. "He's not your average G.I. Joe, is he?"

Monica says, "He's so cool, Marcia."

I regard Marcia coldly. "Hello, Marcia." I say. "I think we need to talk." Reaching into my locker, I remove the smelly socks from my running shoes. I figure I'll drop them in a garbage can the first chance I get. I grope around under all the junk in my locker for this combination lock that I brought to school once. We're not supposed to put locks on our lockers, but I'm going to anyway, so nobody will be able to open my locker to get at Joe.

"How did you get him to talk, Marcia?" asks Dana.

"Yes, how did you?" I ask, finding the lock under my sweatshirt.

Joanna Binkley nudges Marcia. "Hey, Marcia, don't

feel bad. Guess who else got a chain letter? Moi."

Joe calls out, "I want to meet everybody!"

Monica introduces everyone. "I'm Monica Quigley," she says. "And this is Dana Erickson, and that's Joanna Binkley."

"Joanna Binkley!" exclaims Joe, perking up.

"You've heard of me?" she asks, greatly surprised.

"Yes. You think you know everything," Joe says, grinning, hoping to charm her.

Joanna Binkley places her hand on top of her head. *"What?"*

"You are a big tub of lard!" Joe says gleefully.

Joanna Binkley blurts out, "Tub of lard!"

Fortunately, and not a minute too soon, the bell for the next class rings.

"Well, Joe, I'll see you in a little while," I say and, with that, quickly close my locker. I place the lock on my locker and snap it shut. "Come on," I say as I'm ushering everyone away. "We'll be late for class. Now remember. Not a word to anyone about Joe."

21.

DURING LUNCH PERIOD, while all the other kids are in the cafeteria, I stay at my locker and feed Joe— that is, I try to. He won't eat any of my tuna fish sandwich. Every time I try to give him a little piece, he turns his head away and says, "Uh-oh!"

"Would you stop saying that!" I order, losing my patience. "Now eat!" I practically have to force a little piece of the sandwich into his mouth. While I am waiting for him to swallow it, Marcia comes up from behind me and taps my shoulder. I nearly have a heart attack. "Don't *do* that!" I cry.

"How's Joe?"

"Thanks for trying to get me in trouble," I say.

"What are you talking about?"

"Why don't you just get on the PA system and tell the whole school about Joe?"

"I only told Dana."

"Yeah?" I say. "What about Monica Quigley?"

"I didn't tell her," says Marcia. "I swear I didn't."

"Here," I say, thrusting my sandwich half into her hand. *You* feed Joe."

I reach into my locker and take out my report on Madame Curie. There is a trail of small, blue footprints wandering over the first page. "Oh, no!" I cry.

"What's the matter?" asks Marcia.

I lift up Joe's right foot, then his left, to examine the bottoms of his shoes.

"What is it?" demands Marcia.

"There must be a leaky pen in my locker and Joe stepped in the dumb ink." I shake my report at Joe. "Oh, Joe, look what you've done! You walked all over my report! I can't hand this in now! It's ruined!" Angry and disgusted, I heave the report back into my locker.

Joe lowers his head in shame. He coughs.

"He didn't mean to, Nicole," says Marcia. "Look, maybe you can . . ." she is saying when she suddenly becomes distracted by something behind me. Turning, I see Tommy Tarentino walking toward us down the corridor. He is a skinny boy with very curly, dark hair.

"Nicole," says Marcia, her eyes following Tommy Tarentino as he walks to his locker on the opposite wall. "Would it be okay if I showed Joe to Tommy Tarentino?"

I shake my head. "Absolutely not."

"Please?"

"No, Marcia. N-O. No!"

"Don't forget you owe me a favor."

I stamp my foot. "Now that's not fair, Marcia!"

"Is that the example you want to set for Joe?" she asks. "That it's okay to break a promise?"

I glance at Joe. He is looking curiously up at me. I groan. "Go tell Tommy Tarentino to come over."

"Thanks, Nicole!" She clutches both hands to her heart and, heaving a dramatic sigh, says, "Be still my heart!"

I roll my eyes. Joe rolls *his* eyes.

Marcia slips a finger into her collar, pulls, and loudly gulps. "Well, here goes nothing," she says and, handing me back my sandwich half (which, I notice, she's taken a few bites out of), she leaves, shuffling her feet along the floor.

I tear off a small piece of the sandwich and put it in Joe's mouth.

"Mommy, what does Marcia mean?" Joe asks.

"Don't talk with your mouth full. What does she mean by what?"

"Be still my heart?"

"Oh, she's just being funny. She's nervous about having to talk to Tommy Tarentino."

"Why?"

"See, Marcia likes Tommy Tarentino. And when a girl likes a boy as much as Marcia likes Tommy Tarentino, her heart does funny things—it beats really fast whenever she's near him."

"Do boys have hearts?"

"Well of course they do."

"Do I have a heart?" he asks. "What is a heart, anyway?"

"A heart is a . . ." I say, pausing. It dawns on me that I have no idea whether a heart is an organ or a muscle. "It's right here," I say, patting my chest. To avoid any further questions that I may not be able to answer, I turn to see what is taking Marcia so long. She has walked past Tommy Tarentino's locker; in fact, she's way down at the far end of the corridor. I motion for her to hurry up. She grimaces, shrugs, and then comes back, walking very, very slowly. The closer she gets to Tommy Tarentino, the slower she walks. She is almost at his locker when, throwing up her arms, she rushes by him.

"I can't do it!" she cries. She looks so disappointed and upset with herself.

I gently touch her on the arm. "I'll do it," I say. I

stride over to Tommy Tarentino's locker and say, "Hi, Tommy."

Tommy swings around. "Well, hello, Nicole!" he says, rather surprised to see me.

"Marcia has something she'd like to show you," I announce. Being nosy, I peek into his open locker. He's got the cleanest locker *I've* ever seen. His books and notebooks are all carefully stacked and a gray sweater is hanging neatly from a hook. A long, narrow box filled with rolls of breath mints is sitting on his shelf. It's the kind of box you'd see displayed in the checkout line of a supermarket. All I can say is Tommy Tarentino must have a terrible problem with bad breath. "Before she shows you what it is, though, you have to promise me one thing," I tell him.

"What's that?"

"You won't tell anybody about it."

"What is *it*?"

"Just promise!"

"Okay! Okay! I promise!"

I bring Tommy Tarentino over to my locker. "Hi," he says to Marcia.

Marcia tries to smile. "Hi!" she squeaks. Marcia opens the locker door, and there, happy as can be, is Joe. "It is a pleasure to meet you!" he says, bowing.

For the longest time, Tommy Tarentino simply stares at Joe. Then he runs his hand through his curly hair and lets out this very unattractive, high-pitched laugh. (What Marcia sees in him is beyond me.)

"It's a G.I. Joe," says Marcia. "He's not your average G.I. Joe, is he?" Marcia sure knows how to run a joke into the ground.

"He's alive!" exclaims Tommy Tarentino, delightedly.

"Isn't he cute?" asks Marcia.

As if on cue, Joe rolls his eyes. Tommy Tarentino laughs. Joe says, "Awesome! Geez Louise!" and "Yeah, right!" Then he slaps his forehead a couple of times.

"Wow!" says Tommy Tarentino. "He's great!"

Marcia is beaming. "Isn't he?" She pats Joe on the head. "His name is Joe."

"What's he doing alive?" asks Tommy Tarentino, speaking in a very quick, excited voice. "I used to have a G.I. Joe doll just like this one. He wasn't alive or anything and he had a beard, but he was the same size. My dad got him at a garage sale. Boy, I had so much fun with him. I used to love to try and pull off his arms and legs. I thought it would be hilarious if I could stick the left leg on where the right leg went and the right leg where the left leg went."

Joe steps back. The color has drained from his face. His jaw has dropped open.

"Then you know what I'd do, I'd take him down to my father's tool room and—" Tommy Tarentino is saying when I push him away from my locker.

"You're a real sicko, you know that!" I cry. I cup

my hand around Joe to try and comfort him. He's trembling. I turn to Tommy Tarentino. "Don't you ever, ever, come near Joe or my locker again." I sound as fierce as Mom sounds when she yells at Matthew after he's done something to make me cry. "And don't you dare breathe one word to anyone about Joe or I'll pull *your* two legs off and put them on the wrong way!"

22.

I AM SO RELIEVED when school is finally over. I really am.

On our way home, Marcia says, "You have to admit, that was pretty funny when Joe told Joanna Binkley she was a big tub of lard." Marcia looks down at my knapsack at Joe. "Nice work, Joe!"

I hold up my hand. "Please. I'd rather not talk about it. I can't tell you how sick I am of kids coming up to me and saying they heard I had a G.I. Joe doll that was alive in my locker."

"It was great, though," says Marcia. "They all thought you were pulling a big Halloween prank on them. Putting that lock on your locker was a stroke of genius. They thought you were making the whole thing up after you refused to show them Joe."

"Well," I say. "I'm just glad school is over and Mrs. Babcock gave me till Monday to hand in my report on Madame Curie."

It's turned into a sunny day. It's so warm out, I have my jacket unbuttoned and Marcia has taken off her parka. A bunch of yellow leaves from a tree we're passing by twirl and flutter down to the sidewalk.

"Hey!" says Marcia enthusiastically, as she hops over a big crack in the sidewalk. "Let's take Joe out trick-or-treating with us. We can dress him up." She bends down and says to Joe, "What do you say, Joe? Want to go out with us on Halloween?"

Joe is sucking on something. "What is Halloween?" he asks, in a garble.

I stop. "Joe, what do you have in your mouth?"

"I think it's a breath mint," Marcia answers. "He can barely fit it in his mouth.

"Where on earth did you get a breath mint, Joe?" I ask.

"Somebody put it in—what is that thing called again?"

"What thing?" I ask.

"You know, the thing I was in."

"My locker?"

"That's it," says Joe. "Somebody put it in your locker."

"Who?" I ask.

"I don't know who. It dropped out of—what are those other things called?"

"What do they look like?" asks Marcia.

"They're really long," he says, holding out his arms wide.

"You mean vents?" I ask.

He shrugs. "Anyway. That's where it came from."

"Who do you think put it in?" Marcia asks me.

"I know who it was," I reply. "Tommy Tarentino."

Gagging, Joe spits out the breath mint.

Marcia's forehead wrinkles. She is distressed. "Tommy Tarentino gave Joe a breath mint! Boy, am *I* jealous!"

Joe coughs. Then he sneezes. Then he coughs again. He sounds kind of congested. I tap him gently on the back with two fingers until he stops coughing. I feel his forehead, saying, "Gee, Joe, I hope you're not coming down with something."

As soon as we get home, I open a can of Campbell's chicken soup and fix Joe a little bowl of it. (Marcia eats the rest.) I'm pretty worried about him. I'd feel just awful if he got sick with something that was going around at school. After Joe finishes his soup, I take him up to the guest room and make him take a nap in his bed. That's what Mom would make me do if I weren't feeling so hot—make me take a nap. Joe falls right to sleep.

"Gosh, I sure hope Joe feels well enough to go out with us on Halloween," says Marcia. She is flopped on the guest room bed. I am sitting cross-legged on the floor beside Joe's aquarium.

"I'm sure he'll be okay after he takes a nap," I say.

"I know what Joe can go out as," Marcia says.

"He can go out as an ear of corn. He's about the right size."

"That's a thought," I say. I don't want to hurt Marcia's feelings, but I think her idea is dumb.

"Well . . ." says Marcia, thinking. "How about a roll of aluminum foil?"

I shrug. "I suppose we can do that if we can't think of anything else."

Marcia looks sore. "What's wrong with that idea?"

"A roll of aluminum foil?" I say, making a face.

"I don't think it's such a bad idea."

"Hey, I know what Joe can be!" I say.

"What, the Pillsbury Doughboy?" Marcia says crossly, in a very condescending voice.

"A California surfer! My old Ken doll has all these surfer clothes he can wear. We can make a surfboard out of cardboard."

Marcia climbs off the bed. "I like my aluminum foil idea better."

I am so excited, I poke Joe in the side to wake him. "Hey, Joe, wake up! Guess what you're going out as? A surfer!"

Joe blinks his sleepy eyes. "A what?"

Marcia walks to the door. "Well, you do as you like. I'm using your bathroom."

I can tell by her attitude that she's annoyed we're not dressing Joe up as a roll of aluminum foil. Well, that's her problem.

110

23.

UP IN THE ATTIC, I set Joe down on a small table that has an old toaster sitting on top of it. I open the toy chest and begin to search for the old shoe box that I used to put Barbie's and Ken's clothes in.

"Are you excited about going out as a surfer?" I ask Joe.

"Yes," he says. "But what is a surfer?"

"It's someone who rides a board on top of big ocean waves." I demonstrate what someone does on a surfboard. Knees bent, feet firmly planted on the floor, I hold out my hands and move my body this way and that as if I am trying to keep my balance.

Joe nods his head understandingly. "Oh, okay!"

I have to really dig around in the toy chest before I come upon the shoe box. Picking through the heap of clothes, I find a flowery bathing suit and a Hawaiian shirt and a straw hat that belong to Ken and a pair of

111

pointy red sunglasses that belong to Barbie. I turn to Joe, but he's disappeared.

"Joe?" I say, glancing about.

Joe pokes his head out from behind the toaster, and waves at me to hurry over.

"Who is that?" he whispers excitedly. He points to where all the dolls are lined up along the windowsill.

"Who?"

"Her!"

"You mean Barbie?"

"Barbie?" he exclaims. "She is pretty!"

"Yes, she is very pretty," I say.

"She is the prettiest girl I have ever seen in my whole life."

"Joe, you've only been alive for a day," I remind him.

"I want to meet her," he says and then he adds, "Pleeeze!"

"Sure, if you want to," I say. I turn to the window. "Barbie, I'd like you to meet—"

"Mommy, wait!" Joe cries wildly. "Tell her I'm cute. Okay?"

"Well of course I will," I reply, doing my best to keep from giggling. "Barbie, I'd like you to meet Joe—who's so cute you won't believe it."

Joe, looking very earnest, steps out from behind the toaster. Head held high, arms swinging, he marches out to the edge of the table. With a majestic

sweep of his arm, he bows to Barbie. "It is a pleasure to meet you," he announces.

He stares at her, smiling broadly, waiting for a re-
sponse. "It is a pleasure to meet you!" he says again
a moment later, only much louder. Apparently, he
thinks Barbie is hard of hearing.

His smile fades when, once again, she doesn't re-
spond. He looks at me, befuddled.

I shrug. I'm afraid if I say anything I'll break up
with laughter.

Turning back to Barbie, Joe cocks his head. He
rolls his eyes. He says "Awesome!" Then he says
"Geez Louise!" and "Yeah, right!" Then he sticks his
finger into his coller, pulls, and swallows loudly. He
is getting more and more flustered. He can't figure
out why she isn't laughing or saying, "He's *so* cute!"

He turns to me, almost in tears. "Mommy, why doesn't Barbie talk?" he asks miserably.

I suddenly realize that I've taken this thing much too far. "Oh, Joe, she's only a doll," I say, rushing over to hold him. "Dolls can't talk. So don't worry about it. Really. Now here. Try this on." I fit the sunglasses on him. They look absolutely hysterical.

"What are these?" he asks, taking the sunglasses off.

"Leave them on. They're called sunglasses." I hear Marcia coming up the attic stairs. The instant Marcia sees Joe in the sunglasses she bursts out laughing. "Who's that dashing man?" she asks.

I place the straw hat on Joe's head. "What do you think of Ken's hat?" I ask Marcia.

"Who's Ken?" asks Joe.

"That's Ken over there next to Barbie," Marcia says. "He's Barbie's boyfriend."

"What is a boyfriend?" asks Joe.

"Oh, you know, a sweetheart," explains Marcia, with a wave of her hand. "Someone a girl likes very much."

"Barbie likes *him*?" asks Joe.

"Well, I should say so!" cries Marcia. "They've been an item for—gee, I don't know. What would you guess, Nicole? Ages, anyway."

"I can't believe Barbie likes *him*!" says Joe, flabbergasted. He pulls off Ken's hat in disgust and flings

114

it over the edge of the desk. "I'm not wearing Ken's hat!"

"What's got into Joe?" Marcia asks, puzzled.

"He's got a crush on Barbie," I reply.

"Ohhh, *that's* cute!" says Marcia.

"C'mon, Joe, don't be a pain," I say as I pick up the straw hat and set it on his head.

He chucks it over the edge again. "No! No! No! I am not wearing Ken's hat!" He rips off the sunglasses, and throws *them* to the floor.

"The roll of aluminum foil is looking better and better every second," Marcia remarks.

"Joe," I say, paying no attention to her. "Don't you want to be a surfer?"

"No!"

I try to think of how I can change his mind. "See this orange convertible, Joe?" I ask, picking up Barbie's car from the toy chest. "It's Barbie's. If you go out as a surfer, *you* can drive around in it!" I try to make it sound like it's a very big deal.

Joe gapes at the car. "Barbie has her *own* orange convertible!" He drops to his knees and pleads, "Barbie! Barbie! Pleeeze, I beg you, just give me a chance. I know you'll like me better than Ken." He looks hopefully at Barbie. The sight of her coldly gazing off into the distance is just too much for Joe. He buries his face in his hands and sobs. "How can she like that—that—that real dork?"

115

I would try to calm him, but it's been a long day, I'm tired, and I'm at the end of my patience. "Come on, Joe, I told you. She's only a doll! So will you please do as you're told and put on this darn hat so I can see what you look like?"

Marcia butts in then. "Oh, Nicole, why don't you just leave Joe alone?"

I glare at her. "Why don't you just shut up, Marcia!"

"Why don't you? You know, I'm sick and tired of you bossing me around. You're a big bully!"

I'm about to say "Yeah, right!" but I catch myself. "I don't boss you around."

"Oh, no, you don't boss me around," Marcia replies, in a very unpleasant voice.

"You're giving me a real headache, you know that, Marcia?" I say. "Maybe you should leave."

"Hey, my pleasure!" she says. She picks up Joe. "And just so you can't bully Joe around anymore, I'm taking him with me."

"Oh no you're not!" I say, grabbing Joe out of her hands. Joe, cowering, shields his face with his hands. "He's staying here with me." I give her a push. "Now get out of this house!"

"Hey, forget about going out with me tonight!" she says. "And you can forget about me ever being your friend, too!" Swinging around, she storms out of the attic.

116

I run down the attic stairs and hurry through the bedroom hallway until I reach the stairs that lead down to the front door. Marcia is by the front door, throwing on her parka. She pulls on her dorky hat. As she steps out of the house, I call out, "I wouldn't be your friend if you paid me a hundred billion dollars!"

24.

IN A HUFF, I stalk into the guest room with Joe grasped tightly in my hand.

"Okay," he says in a quick, frightened voice. "I'll be a surfer."

"It's too late," I answer, fuming, practically dropping him into his aquarium.

"But I want to be a surfer. Really, Mommy."

"And I said it's too late. You had your chance."

He coughs. "Pleeeze let me," he begs.

"No!" I reply.

"But I didn't know *this* was going to happen!" he wails.

"Well, now you know."

A tear slides down his cheek. He rubs his eyes with his fists. He coughs. Suddenly I feel just wretched for being so mean. I crouch down and say in a soft voice, "I'm sorry, Joe. I shouldn't have yelled at you."

"It's okay, Mommy," he says.

I feel like hugging him, he's so kind and forgiving. "Boy," I say, "I wish I had *you* for a brother instead of Matthew. There's not a mean bone in your whole body. Actually, come to think of it, I don't think you have *any* bones in your body. Anyway, Joe, I'm really sorry I yelled at you. It's just been a long day and I'm tired."

"I know what you mean, Mommy," says Joe. "I'm tired, too."

"Oh, you poor thing," I say and put him into his bed. I can't help noticing as I'm tucking him in just how sick he looks. His eyes are watery and his face looks quite pale.

"Gee, Joe, you don't look so good," I say.

"I don't feel so good," he admits as the phone

rings. I let it ring, waiting for the answering machine to click on. But it doesn't. The phone rings and rings and rings. Mom must've forgotten to turn on the machine. "Oh, for goodness sakes!" I exclaim. "I'll be right back, Joe. Try to sleep."

I race down to Mom's bedroom. "Hello?" I say, all out of breath, into the receiver.

"Hello, may I speak with Nicole Petruzzi, please," says a strange woman's voice.

"This is Nicole."

"Hello, Nicole," says the woman. "This is Mrs. Binkley—Joanna Binkley's mother."

"Oh," I say. "Hello."

"Joanna came home from school today with a wild story about a G.I. Joe doll that she said you had brought to school. She said it was alive."

I blurt out, "She did?"

"Now, Joanna doesn't tell lies, and I was wondering if you might be able to tell me a little something about this G.I. Joe doll."

"Well . . ." I say. I am just about to hang up when I hear myself say, "I can't believe Joanna thought it was really alive. Gee whiz. I guess my ventriloquism is better than I thought."

"You're a ventriloquist?" says Joanna Binkley's mother.

"Well, I'm not very good at it," I reply. "But I try."

Joanna Binkley's mother laughs. "You must be better than you think."

"I guess I am," I say, laughing.

"That Joanna," says her mother. "What a gullible girl she is."

"She sure is," I say, as if I think she is really cute. (Actually, I feel like throwing up.) "Well, tell her I say hello."

"Would you like to talk with her?"

"Oh, no, that's okay."

Joanna Binkley's mother thanks me, we say good-bye, and hang up. I am on my way out of Mom's bedroom when the phone rings again. I am not going to pick it up—for all I know, Joanna Binkley called the Channel 7 Eyewitness News team about Joe—but then I do. "Hello?"

There is a ghoulish, sinister laugh at the other end. "Hi, Matthew," I say, unamused.

"How did you know it was me?"

"What do you want?"

"Tell Mom I won't be home for dinner tonight." Then he adds, in a deep, Dracula-like voice, "I am going out tonight!"

"Okay," I say. "Good-bye."

Matthew keeps talking. "If Mom's not home when you go out, make sure you leave a note. I don't want her blowing a fuse like she did last night."

"I'm not going out," I say.

"How come?" he asks. "I thought you were going out with Marcia."

"Well, you're wrong."

"Why aren't you going out?"

"I had a fight with Marcia, okay?"

"Oh, Nicole, don't be so stupid," he says. "Marcia's your best friend."

"Oh, thanks for telling me," I say, and hang up.

25.

BEFORE RETURNING to the guest room, I go into Mom's bathroom and get an aspirin and a small paper cup. I bite the aspirin into little pieces and spit them into my palm. Then I tear the paper cup to make it smaller, and fill it with cold water.

"Here, Joe," I say, and hand him one of the aspirin pieces. "Take this."

"Where should I take it?" he asks.

"No, I mean, swallow it. It'll make you feel better." I hold out the cup of water. "Here's water to wash it down with."

The moment Joe puts the aspirin into his mouth, he spits it out. "I don't like aspirin, Mommy."

"You're not supposed to like it, silly."

Joe shakes his head. "I don't want aspirin."

"But it'll make you feel better," I tell him. "Now come on." I hold the aspirin out in the palm of my hand, but he pushes my hand away. Then he starts to cough again.

It is very distressing to see him getting so sick. I could kick myself for taking him to school. I really could. I'm trying to think of something nice I can do for Joe when I remember that when Matthew and I were little, Dad used to read to us before we went to bed. We loved it. We'd always take turns: One night Dad would read in Matthew's bedroom, the next night in mine. Dad would sit on the edge of the bed, reading, with Matthew and I, dressed in our pajamas, sitting on each side.

"Where are we going?" Joe asks as I pick up the aquarium.

"You'll see," I say.

I carry the aquarium up the stairs to the attic and set it down on a foot stool. Then I go over to the bookshelf where we keep all the old books nobody reads anymore. The bottom shelf holds the children's books. Scanning the bindings, I pick one of my favorites: *The Story of Ferdinand.* I take a seat on a black-and-white television set and start to read to Joe. Although it's been years since I last read it, I know the story by heart, just about. It feels wonderful to read it again. I can almost hear Dad's voice reading it to Matthew and me. I hold up the book so Joe can see the pictures. I'm only on the fifth page when Joe interrupts me.

"Mommy, if someone had a scar on his face, would you still like him?"

"Of course I would," I reply. "Why do you ask?"

"I was just wondering."

"You think Barbie doesn't like you because of your scar, don't you?"

Joe emphatically shakes his head. "Oh, no, I don't think that."

"Joe," I say. "I keep telling you. Barbie is a doll— she doesn't think or feel anything."

"Ken doesn't have a scar on his face," says Joe.

"Ken is a doll, too," I say.

"*He* is?" Joe cries. "*That's* why she likes him!"

"You're a doll, too, Joe."

"No, I am not," he says sorrowfully.

"Why aren't you a doll?"

"You said dolls don't feel anything. I feel something. I feel something right here," he says, forlornly, and touches the spot where his heart would be.

"Ohhhh, poor Joe!" I cry. "Well, Joe, all I can say is, if Barbie doesn't have enough brains to see what a cute little guy you are, it's her loss. I mean, hey, if I were Barbie, I'd like you much better than Ken."

Joe smiles, turns bright red, and pulls the covers up over his face.

26.

I AM STILL reading Joe his story when I hear a tiny snore. Looking over, I see that Joe is fast asleep. I'm glad he's fallen asleep. Maybe he'll feel better when he wakes up. I pull the little towel over him, and place the screen on top of the aquarium.

On my way downstairs, I hear the front door bell ring.

A little girl and an even littler boy—a witch and a devil—are standing on the front doorstep. I act like I'm really scared.

"Trick or treat!" they scream, holding out their shopping bags.

For the rest of the afternoon and into the evening, Joe sleeps while I hand out candy (dinky Milky Ways this year) to all the kids who come to the door. When I'm not climbing up the attic stairs to look in on Joe, I'm glancing at the clock in the kitchen and wondering where Mom could be. I want to tell her about Joe and ask her what medicine we should give him to make him better. I'm kind of annoyed that she's not home at her usual time.

Finally, at close to seven thirty, Mom comes in the front door.

"Where is everyone?" she calls out. I can tell by the tone of her voice that she is in a perfectly rotten mood. All my anger vanishes.

"Hi, Mom," I say, hesitantly, from the top of the stairs. "You're home late."

"I had to work late," she answers, irritably, tossing her leather briefcase onto a chair. She takes off her coat and hangs it in the front hallway closet. "How come you're not dressed to go out for Halloween?"

"I'm not going out." Then I add, "Marcia isn't feeling well."

"That's too bad," says Mom, who sounds more distracted than genuinely sorry. She is examining the mail she brought in. Mulligan is just outside the front door, meowing to be let in. Mom opens the door, and the cat, still meowing, hurries inside. "You don't want to go out by yourself or call one of your other friends?" Mom asks.

"Not really," I reply. I'm waiting for the right moment to tell her about Joe. I wish she weren't in a bad mood. I just know she'll say something like: See, I told you Joe was going to be a big responsibility.

"Here's a letter for you," Mom says.

"Who could be writing me?" I ask in astonishment as she hands me a letter without a postage stamp. I recognize Marcia's handwriting on the white envelope the moment I see it. She must have put it in our mailbox. I tear open the envelope. It's the chain letter. At the top of the page, Marcia has made a minor adjustment to the *Dear Friend* part. She's put an *Ex* in front of *Friend.* She's also added a quote to the bottom of the page.

> "If I were you, I'd send them to people
> I thought really deserve them."
>   —Nicole Petruzzi
>   October 31

Just then, Mom says, "Oh, for crying out loud!" She is reading a letter. She looks up at me. "Where is Matthew?"

"He called and said he wouldn't be home for dinner."

"Did he say where he was?"

"Uh-uh," I answer. "He just said he was going out."

Enraged, Mom marches down the hallway and into the kitchen, and I decide that maybe I'd better go back upstairs. I hear Mom pick up the phone, dial, and say, "Hello, Dorie?" Dorie is Stringbean's mother. She and Mom are good friends. "Matthew isn't there, is he?" Mom sighs—meaning, no, he's not. "Boy, I can't wait to get my hands on that boy! I just received a letter from the vice-principal who says he's failing three subjects! Three subjects!" she exclaims, in an I've-had-it-up-to-here voice.

27.

As I'm climbing the attic stairs to check on Joe again, I find myself feeling kind of sorry for Mom. Boy, it must be tough taking care of Matthew. I've only had to look after Joe for a day, and *I'm* exhausted.

Joe is still asleep. The little towel that was on his body has fallen off and is lying in a heap by his side. As I place it back on him, I happen to touch his legs. I nearly shriek. They are as stiff as boards.

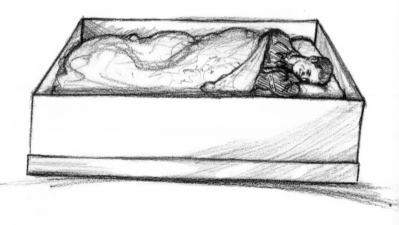

"Oh, no!" I cry, shaking him awake. "Joe, you're turning back into a doll!" Joe, blinking, looks at me with these glazed eyes.

"Oh, gosh, what should I do?" I say in a panic. "The formula must be wearing off!"

I leap up, throw open the toy chest, and pull out the Mr. Chemistry set. Then I race down to the second floor bathroom and frantically grab the Pepto-Bismol and the Head & Shoulders and all the other things I think I used in the formula.

Back in the attic, my hands tremble as I mix the different ingredients. I rack my brain trying to recall just how much of each one I used. When I think I finally have it, I hold the test tube up to the lightbulb on the ceiling. It is the same soft, bluish color of the original formula. I help Joe to sit up, then I raise the test tube to his lips. He takes a couple of gulps, and I lay him back down. I wait, clenching my fists, praying that Joe makes a miraculous recovery.

A minute passes. He looks as sick as ever. I delicately touch his body. Now Joe is stiff from the waist down.

"Oh, jeepers!" I exclaim, fighting back tears. I dump the formula on the floor and start again. I can hardly hold the test tube steady, my hands are shaking so. I deliberately change the amounts of each ingredient I put in so it will be different from the last batch. This time when I make Joe drink the formula, more of the formula dribbles down Joe's chin than goes into his mouth. I wait, my fingers crossed, my eyes closed as tight as I can close them. I am trying to will Joe back to life.

At last I open my eyes. There is a blank look in Joe's eyes and on his face. He doesn't move. The color of his face is no longer pale—it is the color it was when he was a doll. I am too afraid to touch him.

"Joe?" I say timidly.

There isn't a flicker of life in his face.

I feel a lump growing in my throat. "Joe?" I say again, quietly. I reach over to touch his hand.

It is a hard plastic doll's hand once again.

28.

SUDDENLY I'M BAWLING. I'm a real basket case. I pick Joe up and clutch his stiff little body to my chest.

It takes me forever, but I finally get hold of myself. I give Joe a big, wet kiss on the forehead. Then I take Ken off the windowsill and place Joe beside Barbie. I smile to myself, seeing the two of them together, thinking how delighted Joe would be at being so close to Barbie. I fling dumb old Ken halfway across the attic. Joe would have been proud of me.

I stand. The only thing I want to do is go down to Mom's bedroom and call Marcia. She should be the first to know the sad news. Boy, does our fight seem dumb now.

I'm leaving the attic when I hear Mom shouting downstairs. "You know what, Matthew? I've had it! I've had it! *I've had it!*"

133

I stop, my stomach knotting up, my heart pounding.

"Oh, shut up, Mom!" Matthew shouts back.

"Don't you dare say shut up to me!"

"Shut up!"

I practically fly down the stairs. Mom and Matthew are in the kitchen. Mom is standing, hands on her hips, by the sink. Matthew is by the refrigerator, arms folded. "Stop it!" I shriek. "Stop it this instant both of you!"

Mom and Matthew swing around. They look shocked.

"There's too much fighting in this dumb house!" I scream. "Why can't we all just get along and be happy? I just want us to be happy!" I am blubbering now.

Mom tries to put her arms around me, but I won't let her. I run upstairs to my bedroom and throw myself facedown on my bed. A few moments later, Mom is seated on the bed beside me, rubbing her hand on my back.

"Stop crying, honey," she says gently. "We'll stop. We'll stop fighting."

I tilt my face toward her and try to tell her about Joe, but I choke on the words.

"What?" she asks. She reaches over to my desk, pulls two tissues from the Kleenex box, and hands them to me. I wipe my eyes and blow my nose. Matthew, I've just realized, is standing in the doorway with his hands in his pockets, watching us.

"Joe's dead!" I blurt out. "He's turned back into a doll!"

Mom tries to comfort me, but I'm so upset, I don't hear a word she says. I push my face into my pillow and sob.

The next thing I know, the bedroom is dark and Mom and Matthew are gone. I've been sleeping in my clothes. There is a blanket on top of me. I can hear voices from the TV coming up the heating duct. I feel numb and just plain awful. I know something dreadful has happened but I can't remember what. And then I do.

I switch on the lamp by my bed and get up. It's nine o'clock already. I have to talk to Marcia. I have to tell her about Joe.

I call Marcia from the phone in Mom's bedroom. Waiting for somebody to answer, I hold the phone to my ear and gaze at myself in the full-length mirror on the back of the closet door. I look horrible. I really do. My hair is all over the place, my face is puffy, and my eyes are red and glistening. I'm about to turn away when I notice a button pinned to my turtleneck. I stare at it in amazement. It's Matthew's STOP THE ARMS RACE, NOT THE HUMAN RACE button. He must have put it on me while I was sleeping. I touch the button. I'm shocked. I didn't think Matthew could be

nice. I guess I don't know him as well as I thought I did. Maybe it's because of the button or maybe it's because I'm just about to talk to Marcia or maybe it's a little of both, but all of a sudden I don't feel quite so bad anymore.

"Hello? Hello?" Marcia's mother is saying on the other end of the wire.

I brush my hair back with my hand and say, "Hi, Mrs. Schwartz. Could I please speak to Marcia?"